The Tea Ceremony

Also by Gina Berriault

Afterwards

The Son

The Descent

The Infinite Passion of Expectation

The Lights of Earth

The Mistress

Women in Their Beds

The Great Petrowski

THE UNCOLLECTED WRITINGS

The Tea Ceremony

GINA BERRIAULT

Shoemaker [SH] Hoard *Washington, D.C.*

Library of Congress Cataloging-in-Publication Data is available.
ISBN: 1-59376-004-3

FIRST PRINTING

Jacket and text design by David Bullen Design

Shoemaker & Hoard
A Division of Avalon Publishing Group Incorporated
Distributed by Publishers Group West

10 9 8 7 6 5 4 3 2 1

contents

Foreword by Leonard Gardner   *vii*

FICTION

The Tea Ceremony   3
The Figure Skater   *11*
Confessions of an Ex-Flea   *17*
The Vault   *25*
Return of the Griffins   *37*

FRAGMENT OF A NOVEL

The Flood Again   *59*

NON-FICTION

The Naked Luncheon   *77*
The Last Firing Squad   *95*
Neal's Ashes   *111*
Watched: The New Student President   *127*
Wendy Ewald   *145*
The Last of Life   *149*
The Essential Rumi   *159*

ON WRITING

Acceptance Speech: The Commonwealth Club   *165*
Almost Impossible   *169*
"Don't I Know You?"   *175*

AFTERWORD

The Achievement of Gina Berriault by Richard Yates   *191*

Foreword

GINA BERRIAULT's collection of thirty-five stories, *Women in Their Beds*, published in 1996, one of the most honored books of the year, widened the audience of a writer who had long been a master of the short story. A practitioner of the art throughout her career, who also produced moving, beautifully written novels — *The Descent, Conference of Victims* (reprinted as *Afterwards*), *The Son,* and *The Lights of Earth* — Gina had an extraordinary command of short fiction. Her sense of drama, form and proportion, her knowledge of the inner lives of her characters, and the sensitivity and precision of her language, all work in unity to brilliantly evocative effect.

Characterization can be the most difficult skill for a writer to acquire, a skill that in many writers remains undeveloped because it requires a gift and because stories can move along without it, carried by plot alone. Gina had a rare sympathetic connection with her characters; she knew their fluctuating emotions, the reasons for their gestures and their reactions to the gestures of others. She could tell a story on so intimate a level that her characters take on a reality at their depths. Describing the subtlest nuances of behavior, she created her characters as events unfolded, blending the interplay of their personalities with a rich visual world in a style that flows like music. She worked at a level of discernment that for a reader can deepen comprehension of his own life and the lives of others.

Gina once said she wrote to understand people. She also said she *had* to write, and this was not a figure of speech. Usually she seemed at her best when she was writing—spirits and energies up, engaged in the work and the whole process of living. Of course she had days of frustration, but writing filled a fundamental need of her spirit, and she believed creativity not used turned destructive, not least to the self. Out for a walk to take a break from hours at her desk, she could sometimes pass friends and loved ones without noticing them, her mind still involved in her work. One friend who encountered her on these walks said he could see she was always writing. Her concentration had staying power. She put in long days to bring her writing to the standards she set for herself, frequently going on late into the night. On completing a draft, she would often start in on the next draft without so much as a moments pause.

Shy, protective of her privacy and the solitude she needed for her work, Gina was also talkative, humorous, kind, and spontaneously responsive to others and to experience. The vitality of her mind and spirit sparked fascinating conversations. Her mind seemed seldom to rest. Her sensitivity was obvious, yet she had courage, stamina, great tenacity and strength of will. A tragic undercurrent flowed in her view of the world. Awareness of life's preciousness and precariousness seemed ingrained in her. Her allegiance was to the underdog, the rejected and the overlooked.

Gina's greatest strength was in writing about women, but some of her most memorable characters are male. The first Berriault story I came across was "The Stone Boy," about a boy who accidentally kills his brother, and it is unforgettable. I read it some months before I met Gina in San Francisco. "The Stone Boy" brought her recognition as an important talent in the short story and established her territory of the outsider, a territory she never abandoned and to which she returned again in "The Tea Ceremony," the opening story in this volume. It was one of her last works.

Gina believed that others' lives are more deserving of attention than the writer's life. She used autobiographical material infrequently, but in "The Tea Ceremony" she reveals some of the formative forces of her youth: the pity and sadness for a family cast adrift—a once vivacious mother going blind, a brilliant father crushed by the Depression—rejection, yearning for transcendence, a pondering of the power and enigma of beauty. Everywhere in this economical story, so deceptive in its simplicity, are the roots of the future artist. Gina, born to Latvian and Lithuanian immigrants, grew up in Southern California. Her father died suddenly when she was in her teens, and from necessity she stepped into his job writing and editing a jewelry trade journal and taking on support of the family. Yearning for a different life, she turned to her imagination and taught herself at night how to write fiction.

"Return of the Griffins" was her first published story, a tale of spiritual crisis on the world stage of Cold War politics, a powerful, lucid work of imagination and moral commitment. In it an emissary to the United Nations is ushered into an earlier realm of human consciousness wiser and more sane than that of his own time.

"Confessions of an Ex-Flea" is a work from the sixties about an outsider utterly beyond the pale, who dares to pursue a dream of transformation among the Beats and existentialists. Gina's readers may be intrigued to see her comic side given free rein here.

In "The Vault,"a look at art and immortality, published here for the first time, an obscure novelist is led to reflect on the meaning of his years of writing. A one-character story, "The Vault" expands into a satire of American culture. Readers of *Women in Their Beds* will recognize this character, here named Villalba, a librarian, as a precursor of the librarian Perera in "Who Is It Can Tell Me Who I Am?," written nearly three decades afterwards. Gina had never been satisfied with "The Vault" and put it aside, intending to work more on it. When she finally returned to it, she took only the character, the colorful, winningly embittered librarian-novelist, and put him in an entirely new story with a homeless habitué of the San Francisco Public Library. For those interested in seeing how this story provided the seed for the other, it should reveal something about the author's inventive resources. But mostly "The Vault" has been included because it is a pleasure to read.

Chekhov was a writer Gina esteemed without reservation, almost like a beloved friend. She kept a framed photo of him on a bookshelf. Stories such as "Ward 6," "The Woman with the Dog," and "The Black Monk" came up in our conversations numerous times over the years we were together, and there is a certain logic to the Black Monk, a hallucination in Chekhov's story, appearing in the fantasies of the dying revolutionary, Inessa Armand, in Gina's "The Figure Skater." This was one of Gina's final stories, a strange, poetic, hauntingly urgent rendering of inner life as it flares up before ending. She had been reading about Inessa Armand, and I imagine her writing this late at night, thinking about Russia, thinking that Armand would have read Chekhov. And so the Black Monk, a flying figure of legend, found his way, like a figure floating in a painting by Chagall, into this dreamlike story.

"The Flood Again" is from an unfinished novel, one of Gina's last projects. It involves a young woman, "Magda," who meets a very high ranking Washington politician attending the annual summer retreat and revelry at the Bohemian Grove, that extremely private Northern California club whose members are among the most powerful men in American politics, industry and finance. Gina once researched the Bohemian Grove for a magazine article and, if I remember correctly, was the only woman journalist ever allowed on the grounds of that all-male sanctuary. In the planned novel, "Magda's" susceptibility to the politician, with all his power and status, would be in conflict with her own political views. An amateur actress in the beginning of the story, she would in the following years establish herself in movies. An important character was to be her brother, an author committed to exposing oppression in Latin America. The title Gina had chosen for the novel was *The Blue Lit Stage,* the actual name of a torture chamber in a Latin American country. Eventually "Magda" would visit that country to search for her brother who, during his investigations of government torture, would have disappeared. Gina never got to the heart of the story, and this section, the first chapter, is all that she prepared for publication.

Also included in this collection are Gina's distinguished non-fiction pieces. Four were published in *Esquire* during the sixties and seventies. Because of the quality of the writing, and their perception and vision, they remain valuable documents of the period and engaging reading. To my knowledge Gina was the first to write an article for a national magazine about the startling new phenomenon of topless nightclubs in San Francisco, which were drawing hordes of tourists and locals to North Beach during the early days of the sexual freedom movement. "The Naked Luncheon" is made vividly immediate by the story-telling instincts and skills Gina brought with her from her fiction. *Esquire* was showcasing the "new journalism" at that time, personal journalism employing the techniques of fiction, and Gina, who had a number of short stories appear in the magazine, did some outstanding work in that movement.

Written with passion and an eloquent freedom, "The Last Firing Squad" transcends the article form. Through its focus on the bleak Utah landscape, laymen executioners, and a sense of unquestioned lives, it arrives at the bleakness and madness somewhere in the depths of humanity. An incantatory passage recounting the tools of the executioner's trade is devastating. As long as capital punishment continues, this essay won't be dated.

Carolyn Cassady seemed ready to unburden herself of some surprisingly frank disclosures in "Neal's Ashes." Carolyn was the former wife of Neal Cassady, the man Jack Kerouac made into a Beat icon by using him as the model for free spirit Dean Moriarty in *On the Road*. We used to see Cassady around North Beach. After his burnout and death, Gina decided to get the ex-wife's side of the legend; and the final days of Cassady were even sadder than Kerouac's.

David Harris, profiled in "Watched: The New Student President," made news as a leader of the Vietnam anti-war movement who was elected student body president of Stanford University, becoming a symbol of radical youth of the sixties. The article brings back those days of commitment and demonstrations and, in Harris, captures the intelligence, idealism and maturity of a young activist. After it appeared, Harris served a twenty-month prison term for refusing induction. In the years following, he worked as an international journalist, authored a number of books — on the Vietnam War, prison, politics and activism — and is currently back in the news as a spokesman for the revitalized anti-war movement.

It may have been easy for some *Esquire* readers to pass over "The Last of Life," as easy as the general indifference to the elderly that Gina was addressing. But this exceptionally aware and compassionate piece should not be missed. Gina could make a reader care about her cast of characters, even the bit players retrieving newspapers from trashcans.

In her essay "Almost Impossible," Gina says she hoped she would never lose the delusion that kept her writing. She never did, if a powerful drive to create art can be considered a delusion. Maybe Villalba, the librarian-novelist of "The Vault," would call it that. Part of what drove Gina was conscience, the need to serve her talent, to use her gift and her time on earth as meaningfully as she could. Writing seemed inseparable from her identity. To a great degree she was what we find in her pages. Once I asked her about the source of her motivation, and her explanation had a characteristic purity. She said she wanted to make a contribution.

Gina wrote with undiminished dedication until the end of her life. On one of her last days, with her daughter, Julie, reading the galleys aloud, Gina was able to make the final corrections to her fable, *The Great Petrowski,* which she had illustrated with graceful drawings.

It was said of Gina's stories that "the light she casts into the inner recesses of apparently ordinary people makes one feel that

there is no such thing as an ordinary person." And that was the
way she saw things. Her work has heart. She was drawn to survivors of loss, who learn the terms of life and how to continue.
Love in all its trials, death, hope, obsession, lost illusions, wisdom gained or missed — these are some of her themes, which she
handled with virtuosity and great honesty. Gina made her highly
individual contribution to American writing, a contribution that
shimmers with original sensibility. Sensibility begets sensibility;
this is the source of our faith in literature. It is the writers who
deepen our lives who survive. Gina Berriault is among them.

Leonard Gardner, 2003

fiction

The Tea Ceremony

For my true friend,
Isaac Babel,
in his basement.

OCEAN LINERS sailed right on through the Depression years, and certain persons who had jobs, like teachers, could go and visit countries that were not at war. Miss Furguson had been to Japan. She brought to school a silk kimono purchased in Naga-saki, for a sum she would not divulge. One of the boys asked her outright, but she bowed her head, smiling tolerantly. It's not polite to ask those kinds of questions, she said, so we don't answer them. The boy, humiliated, angry, turned his whole body side-ways in his seat and stared out the window.

The kimono hung on a long bamboo rod with a black silk tas-sel at each end, showing off the wide sleeves to advantage and the hand-painted scene of a teahouse and white cranes wading in a stream. It had a red silk lining. You could file along before it but you could not touch it. Miss Furguson fingered the silk between her thumb and forefinger. The feel of silk, nothing like it, she said.

Only for Jolie Lotta, as she filed by, did Miss Furguson point out the kimono's many precious details. What a beautiful girl she was, Jolie Lotta. How pale and clear her skin, how long and light her hair, how modestly plump her hands, ready for those gold rings promising bliss, her bare legs ready for skin-pale silk stockings, her complete person like a presentation of a virtue for all to see. A girl held in such high esteem by Miss Furguson, the boys kept their distance. And how could it be that Jolie Lotta was best friends with me?

Tall dry weeds and wild oats — that was the outskirts of the town and its empty lots, but you'd be surprised by who you'd find in the drugstore. Jolie Lotta's mother was the most beautiful woman I had ever seen in all my thirteen years of learning what beauty is. Hers was beyond comparison with the pretty ones in our class, already preening themselves for their entry into the marketplace. She wore a clerk's tan uniform, her hair, a darker blonde than her daughter's, was coiled at the nape of her neck, and her large, hazel eyes held a certainty of her own beauty, a lovely basking, a look that I hoped I might show for myself someday and knew I never could.

My mother, said Jolie Lotta to me one day, wants me to stop being friends with you. She named three girls who went around together and with nobody else, one whose father was the mayor, one whose father was the city attorney, and one whose father was simply rich, and it was these three girls whom her mother wanted for her friends. I already knew what was unfavorable about me, but I knew more emphatically then. I became who I was in her mother's beautiful eyes. Beauty can do that to you. I became the girl who Jolie Lotta's mother saw, those few minutes in the drugstore when she appeared to be seeing only her daughter. How skinny my legs, how scrawny my hands, still an agile child's hands, sun-browned, stained with colored inks, and how unruly my dark hair, and how crazily stitched my clothes by my mother going blind and insisting on sewing up the tears. With the prescience some children have of their life to come, I knew then that I would keep my own distance from them, from those who were perfected by their beauty and by everybody's adoration. The farther the distance, the less the longing to be like them.

Miss Furguson asked the class to point to the one among us who we liked the best. I pointed to the girl who was a better artist than myself, and found their fingers pointing at me. A mistake! I was entangled hand and foot in Miss Furguson's mistaken question. They would not have chosen me had they known everything about me, the shameful things that only I knew. Oh, is it Delia? said Miss Furguson, not looking at me, looking around to see if some fingers were pointing at some others, and found that they were. Ah hah, this country is a democracy, she said, and smiled at me consolingly.

Noontime, I began to go around alone, seeking places from where I could not see the promenading girls, all perfecting themselves. Then the shyest girl in class, who was never heard from, began to follow me around. She spoke not one word, that Wilma, her large, darkly shining eyes doing all the pleading of me to be her best friend. Go away, I said. Go away and stay away. She would not go, she would not let me be alone. Until one day I pounded on her back, and then she went away. And even as I had thought I was the boy who asked Miss Furguson the price of her kimono, I thought I was that girl, that Wilma. I did not want to be them. It was no place for me to be, there in their wounded hearts, but there I was.

One morning, the moment the bell rang, we went quickly into the classroom, wanting to impress Miss Furguson with our eagerness to obey rules. Jolie Lotta's mother was in the headlines of the town newspaper, caught at doing something disastrously wrong, something against the strictest of all rules. Adrianna Lotta, a divorced woman, living with her mother and thirteen-year-old daughter, Jolie, in the Maple Apartments on Bee Street, was found near death at the side of her lover, City Councilman Mack McPorter, a married man, in the Seaside Motel. Asphyxiated by a leaking gas heater, they were both rescued from death in the nick of time. Our eyes alight, we sat down at our desks. Jolie Lotta was absent.

Miss Furguson, of course, knew more than we knew about this event. It was expected of teachers to know more about any event. She said nothing, but what she knew about this one filled out her person, elevating her short stature, swelling her bosom, enriching her voice, giving us a more complete picture of her than we'd ever had, and that usual stance of hers when she faced us, legs close together, feet close together, became curiously noticeable. Entranced, we watched her every move.

Some persons are made more perfect by what befalls them, as if whatever befalls them can never make them less, can never bring them low, as it might others. I figured this out in the five days Jolie Lotta was absent. I'd glance up at Miss Furguson engrossed at her desk and suspect her of perfecting Jolie Lotta ever more. One morning she was with us again, slipping in, paler, less spirited. The girls who had taken her into their circle enclosed her again, a prize.

Not many days after Jolie Lotta's return, Miss Furguson showed us the Japanese tea ceremony. Set before us were two round black cushions with a shimmer to them, so they must be silk, and a low, lacquered table. On the table was a pale green teapot, so precious you felt undeserving of the sight of it, and two little pale green bowls. While we were out at afternoon recess, Miss Furguson had set things up, to surprise us. On her desk was a bouquet of little yellow flowers in a vase. It had not been there before.

She stood before us, facing us, happier than we had ever seen her. The tea ceremony, she said, is perfectly beautiful, as you will see. If Miss Furguson had seemed happy a few other times, those times were not so believable as this. If whatever you call beautiful makes you happy, then that's what beautiful things are for, I thought, especially if they belong to you. I wish, said Miss Furguson, that I could have given each of you a nice clean hand-kerchief to wipe your hands with before you entered this tea-room. If we were really in Japan, she said, that's what we'd do. I've invited Jolie Lotta to do the honors. We've rehearsed it together and we're pretty confident.

Then Jolie Lotta came forward and knelt down on a cushion, her bare knees touching the floor. She bowed her head to Miss Furguson, who knelt down, less easily, on the other cushion, and there they were, facing each other, their profiles to the class. I thought I might draw their picture together, later, as a way of being an important part of the ceremony, even almost necessary. To begin, said Miss Furguson, we must all admire the teapot and the bowls and even the bamboo whisk. They spent a long minute doing that, Miss Furguson making chirpy sounds of belief, of belief in the beauty of the objects set before them. With a small square of white silk, each one wiped the rim of her bowl so very much cleaner than any common cup was ever wiped. Then Jolie brought up from the floor a small iron kettle that had been wait-ing on a pad. Jolie, said Miss Furguson, is pouring the water slowly, very slowly, into the teapot which contains the green tea powder. Now, she said, Jolie is stirring it with the whisk. Too much stirring will make the tea foamy and too little will make the tea watery, so Jolie is stirring it just right, as you can see. Now the tea is steeping, said Miss Furguson. Then Jolie calmly, graciously, poured tea into Miss Furguson's bowl and into her own bowl, and wisps of steam rose up. How fragrant it is, said Miss Furguson, and they took their time inhaling. Then, at last, at last, they sipped their tea. Perfectly beautiful, said Miss Furguson. How perfect. And I knew that I would never draw them. My pen would make only false moves and the picture give away my lacking and my longing.

Nights at home, I thought about that tea ceremony. If Miss Furguson were ever to visit my family, something she'd never do but something I feared anyway, she'd know the worst if she came at supper time. Her suspicions about us, and I knew she had some, would be confirmed before her eyes. Other families sat down together, while each member of my family ate apart. A family askew, a family alone in a rain-stained bungalow in the weeds, faded curtains from the last house that didn't fit the windows of this one, and my parents' bed a sagging fold-out davenport. My brother, who strode the streets all day or besieged our mother with dreams of fabulous wealth, ate by himself like a lone and hungry wolf, the first to be served by my sister. Over in Japan, he'd scare all those tea worshippers out of their wits. Teacups crashing to the floor, the teapot loudly cracking apart by itself. Our mother, who was served next, who ate more gracefully than anybody I'd ever seen but now sat with the dish in her lap and did not know exactly where in the dish to place her spoon, would never, of course, be invited. Next, my sweet sister and I sat down together, eating our supper just to get it over with, not talking, each knowing enough about what was in the other's unhappy heart. So afraid of making mistakes, my sister would not even be offered a chair where she could sit and watch the ceremony. My father came a long way on the clanking streetcar from the city, from his cluttered little office, and entered quietly, and did not sit down to eat until he had kissed our mother, gently, lovingly, on the top of her head. He placed only one thing at a time on his plate and ate slowly, and his shirt was white, washed and ironed by my sister, and our mother called him noble. My father, I thought, might possibly be acceptable at some celestial tea ceremony in some far distant time. One evening, coming in the door, he caught me doing something I had never done before, kneeling at my mother's slippered feet, begging her to tell me that someday I'd be a somebody. *Tell me, tell me,* I pleaded, and she waved her spoon over my head and said that I would. My father must have known, more than my mother did, what I meant by a somebody. A Somebody out in the world, who'd redeem us all.

One morning Miss Furguson stood up before us and told us something we already knew. We are at war, said Miss Furguson. The Japanese have bombed our territory, they have destroyed our ships, they have killed many of our sailors, and they have done this deceitfully.

The world went awry. It may always have been awry but I hadn't known, being so concentrated on my family awry. The world shattered itself, like that teapot my brother's presence would have caused to crack apart. Everywhere in the world millions of people were dying and great cities were blasted into rubble and dust and families huddled together in basements, hiding down there from inescapable night. Jolie Lotta disappeared from that class and her mother disappeared from the drugstore. I glanced in twice through the display window and could not find her.

Years into the war I began to look for something to call perfectly beautiful. Whatever it was, I couldn't find it again. I heard of a place in another city called a Museum of Art, and I wandered in. Carpets, like sanctification of my otherwise noisy shoes, and fragrance — sandalwood? — throughout the wide spaces, a fragrance I was to return for, again and again, as much as for the objects on their pedestals and in their frames. I stood before each one, or walked around it, at a loss. What I had to do, I saw, was imagine their beauty. What I had to do was dream it up, just what all those artists must have had to do. Wandering around in all that dreamed-up beauty, I thought about Jolie Lotta. How she presided at the tea ceremony, how she stirred the tea and poured it, and inhaled its fragrance, and drank it, and nodded in agreement with Miss Furguson that it was all perfectly beautiful, her own self, too, Jolie Lotta, amidst it all. If you could save yourself from a world awry by calling up something beautiful, I called up Jolie Lotta from my memory. Or I must have called her up from my wounded heart, since, even after so long, I wasn't spared the pain of my lacking and my longing.

The Figure Skater

"MADAME ARMAND?"

Inessa opens her eyes, a task. No one is at her bedside. Someone was there a moment ago—skirts rustling, a cool cloth on her
brow, a wet fingertip trace on her temple. Strangers all around,
lying under thin covers, under only a garment. Carbolic soap
smell, a fly buzzing. Cries and prayers everywhere, muffled by
the thudding fever in her ears.

Children, come to me. Your loveliness was with me always,
everywhere I went, as close to me as my dear comrades. Auntie
of long ago, you come too, come to me again and take my hand in
yours again, just as you did my little gloved hand when we went

together on that long, long train ride from Paris to St. Petersburg, waving goodbye to my last sight of my father, handsome actor waving. Auntie, care for me, look after me.

"Madame Armand?"

She tries to move her lips to say, I live, you see, and someone lays a hand on her breast and her heart leaps up to meet it. I live, you see, her heart says, and someone goes away.

Vladimir Ilyich, you know I'm here in this land of raging cholera, here in the Caucasus, sent with a message I can't recall, my mind's a swamp fire. Come down, spare me a moment, devise a way to rescue me from death. How high into the sky you go and how far you go and how fleet you are, skating your complicated figures just as you told me you did in Siberia in icebound exile, delighting the young peasants. Over the piercing Alps you fly, over the roofs of Zurich, over Prague, over Cracow, thousands of kilometers in an instant, so far away you won't return until morning when Nadya and myself and our comrades sit down under the striped awnings of Cafe Landolt and wait for you to join us.

"Madame Armand?"

Oh what a sad young nurse stands there above me.

Nurse, my dear, are you the one who tended me in Paris when I was a little child and sick? How kind of you to come all that way to tend me again. I am so glad you are still alive and grown younger.

"She speaks in French. What is she saying?"

"One of the aristocrats. They learn their French from their governess."

No, I am not an aristocrat.

"Pray, Madame, and God will save you."

Nurse, I used to pray but I can no longer pray. I have felt so deeply how everyone prays to Him, all suffering Russia is praying to Him, and He does nothing. Look up, Nurse, watch Volodya, the most daring figure skater in all of Russia. You've never seen such marvelous designs in all your life. Is there someone with him, now? Do you see someone flying through the air with him? I see two and I know who's the other, I know and I'll tell you. Sit down by me and remember with me the little story by our sweet Chekhov, the one about the Black Monk who comes flying to earth every thousand years, cassock flapping in the wind, gray beard like a thin cloud blowing, barefoot. And one day he sits down on a bench by the side of the young scholar and they talk together about humanity, about the glorious future our young scholar will bring about. Yes, with his remarkable mind, his persuasive writings, his genius. Such an uplifting conversation, it makes that young man feel so fine, so valuable to the world. Nurse, my dear, it's that Black Monk, that's who's up there with our Volodya. Our sweet Chekhov is up there, too, perched on a roof in the cold night, and he wants to fly with them but he can't, poor soul, he's coughing so badly there's blood on his chest.

"Delirious."

No, I am not, I am not. It's what they said of me, a lady, a rich manufacturer's wife, leaving her family, her husband, throwing in her lot, her life, with the revolutionists. Missions whose dangers now seem as nothing, arrested again and again by the Czar's police. What terrible prison is this? Is this the fortress of Peter and Paul?

"The Saints do listen."

I escaped, I fled to Switzerland and there I joined them, Vladimir Ilyich and Nadezhda, his wife, never parting from them. Such long talks, such long walks, such long days working together, and the nights with him so brief. Nadya like a sister to us. My only hint was something no one will ever read. I'll tell *you*, Nurse, my dear, since yours may be the last young face to look into my own. A popular brochure on love, that's what I was writing, and I said that even the kisses of an ephemeral passion, a liaison, were more pure, more poetic than kisses between crude and loveless mates. And what did Volodya say about that? Inessa, why bring up liaison kisses? Inessa, be logical, why not compare the kisses of a loveless bourgeoisie marriage to the kisses of love in a civil proletarian marriage? Nurse, my dear, you can see why I gave it up, gave up writing of love and kisses, of kisses and kisses, so many kinds of kisses.

Inessa opens her eyes. The sad young nurse is gone, vanished, already aboard the train back to Paris and growing older the closer she gets, an old woman in a jolting compartment, her dry mouth wanting an English mint, wanting cold Alpine water.

"Madame Armand?"

Back so quickly and young again. Nurse, my dear, it's what trains do with our lives, carry us into our lives and carry away our lives. So many trains I've climbed aboard, up the steps with Nadya and Volodya, and into yet another compartment, our few, frayed bags, our precious books piled on the seats beside us, the emigrés' shaking library. Like a traveling rogues' gallery, they're wearing the same clothes year round, his one coat, elbows out, his trousers mended at the seat. Even so, all's clean and tidy. Geneva, come spring, she's painting another coat of varnish on her black straw hat and Volodya is cleaning his bowler with gasoline, and, out in the street in his shirtsleeves, he's making their bicycles shipshape again. Nurse, my dear, you'll laugh in your tender breast when I tell you what I used to imagine. Volodya pedaling his bicycle into the Finlandia station in Petrograd, a red banner flying from the handlebars. We returned by train, you know, a secret coachful of comrades, a train entering a sea of red banners, the Red Sea parting for a train.

"She breathes?"

Nurse, my dear, that black monk flying around up there dropped in on us wherever we were, London, Paris. Volodya throws open the window and in he flies and sits himself down at our table, our table loaded high with our letters, our messages, our bulletins, our newspapers, and Vera Zasulich, awestruck, out of her wits, offers him a cigarette which he refuses, of course, and he talks with us and gestures with us, wisely, widely, and shakes his head with us over the dazzling, beribboned nobility who cannot see him even when his black robes sweep across their eyes. Then Volodya asks me to play the piano for them, and I do, I do, I sit down and play Beethoven's sonatas far into the night.

"Shall we cover her face?"

"No, no, no. Not yet, not yet."

Nurse, look up! The monk is flying in a great circle, spiralling towards a center that seems to be everywhere and now out again into a circle ever wider, so wide its circumference must be nowhere. Do you think he's describing God for us? And now it's Volodya's turn. What astonishing figures no one has ever attempted before! They're shoulder to shoulder now, they're in tune with each other, and off they go. Off they go together, flying over Moscow, over Petrograd, over the spires and domes of those glittering cities, over the moonlit steppes and over the forests' dark masses.

"Can you hear me, Inessa?"

Nurse, my dear, they're flying away from us for good. They're arm in arm, steadfast, dear companions, flying away into this vast pale night, far away into this night without sunset or sunrise, lost among all those slowly bursting stars.

Confessions of an Ex-Flea

My EARLIEST RECOLLECTION is of some animal's soft underfur — no more than a tactual recollection, so I presume that was my larval infancy. That I was able, upon emerging from the stuporous air of the cocoon, to cogitate and to converse came as no surprise. Perhaps if I had been alone in these accomplishments they might have surprised me, but my brother was also talented in this way. Time has proved my intelligence superior to his; but in the beginning it was his similarity to myself that led me to take my talents for granted, and it was his curiosity that led both of us into the genera we occupy today.

The story begins the day my brother swallowed the cat. Before this act he spent many hours meditating upon it. The force that sent him into the actual act was his doubt that it could be done at all. We had been living on a small gray tabby named Murphy, a kitten with a bony face and paw cushions like pomegranate seeds. Snuggled down in Murphy's armpits, we listened while his master read aloud from the writings of those he called the Great Inspirational Dismalists. Often he read passages in which the authors likened man to various vermin. For example, Dostoevsky in *Notes from Underground* refers to himself as a crushed and ridiculed mouse, and Kafka devotes an entire story to the travail of a young man who became a cockroach. We hopped out upon the bare floor to hear this latter one without interference.

There was Murphy's master lying on a mattress on the floor, flat on his back, reading to a trio of young men — one sitting cross-legged on the floor, one lying on the floor with his arms under his head, and the third astraddle a chair. How absorbed they were in this tale of a man who became a cockroach!

Once again in Murphy's fur, we discussed this strange inclination.

"It's too common to be unnatural," said my brother.

"A lot of unnatural behavior is common," I countered.

"All right, let us say it is unnatural," said my brother. "All the better. If human beings indulge their unnatural inclinations, then I, a flea, a creature of instinct, will find a still greater kick in indulging mine. I think that I shall reverse the process, however, for I am very low already, zoologically. I shall become a cat."

We lay very still, attentive to Murphy's heart, to his twitchings, to his cat nature. "Shall I?" my brother asked hoarsely.

"Can you?" I replied.

The next day he did. I skittered up the young man's pants leg and took refuge on top of his head in his unkempt black hair. The facts that my brother had swallowed the cat, and that the young man, bending over to pet him, commented that his head was getting smaller because his body was getting fatter, so that in contour he resembled a flea, were events of such tremendous gravity and portent to me that I came to need my nesty refuge as a Buddhist monk needs his mountain cave.

In the days that followed, I overheard anecdotes and gossip, news releases and classic discourses that were affirmations of my brother's act. It came to me that a lot of swallowing was going on. Something is always swallowing something else, and each becomes the other in a terrific amalgam. Whatever is swallowed becomes the swallower, and the reverse is also true in that the swallower becomes the thing swallowed. Sometimes the contours are changed, sometimes only the expression changes on the face of the swallower or the swallowed.

Since the young man in whose rooms I was living called himself a poet, most of my observations bearing upon this theory are literary. I heard that Kerouac had swallowed an entire generation, the United States from coast to coast, Mexico City, Southern Pacific trains and any woman sitting next to him on a Greyhound bus. Mann swallowed Joseph and all his brothers, Melville swallowed the White Whale, Durrell swallowed Alexandria, Thomas Wolfe swallowed everything he laid his eyes on.

Swallowers outside the literary area also served to confirm my conjectures. A woman visitor was in haste to reveal that she had swallowed unboiled water in remote villages in Central America, and it occurred to me that she was swallowing Life with a loud, exhibitionist gulp. One evening the young man exploded into a laugh while reading the newspaper: he said that the State Department was accusing Fidel Castro of attempting to swallow the Entire Hemisphere. At another time he went around rubbing his hands together prophesying that the sit-inners were going to swallow the South. The sandwich across the counter was only the first bite.

I vowed to venture beyond my existence as a flea and do some swallowing for myself. My brother seemed content as a cat. I watched him bite and scratch at his former comrades and crawl in under the covers with the young man in whose hair I meditated. But I aspired to more than that. He appeared to be absolutely stunned into a state of static vanity by his accomplishment and incapable of the next try, while it seemed to me that only as a human being could I participate in the kind of swallowing that meant something.

One evening a young English friend called upon the young man to bid him goodbye. He was leaving the next morning by jet for London to hold his dying grandfather's hand in the hope of inheriting some acreage on a Caribbean island — acreage necessary, he said, for him to write his novel in. The young poet stared enviously through his dark glasses at the inheritor, but it was not of the island he was thinking. "You going to hop over to Paris and dig the scene with Sartre?" he asked, his mouth filled with disgust for his own condition. Before the visitor left, I had hopped under his overcoat collar.

The choice of just whom to swallow in that grand transmutation into human being was now to torment me. Should it be this young man on his way to England, perhaps to the West Indies and fame as a novelist? But something in me wanted to look a little further, experiencing the anguish of the search. The Search! It came to me, as we were flying over the Atlantic, that perhaps I could swallow Sartre!

After a day in the company of the heir's grandpapa and a night in the company of the heir and his friends celebrating the old man's demise, I concealed myself in the fur collar of a lady who had informed the party of her intention to visit Paris.

As soon as we arrived, the young lady found her way to the room of a male student who at once made her feel at home by throwing her down on the bed. The next day I accompanied him to his classes at Ecole Normale Supérieure and hopped into the pants cuff of a Professor of Philosophy. After spending two weeks with him and his family and their two cats — in whose company I prowled the alleyways of Paris — I was at last conveyed to the apartment of the great man himself. When the Professor had departed, I spoke. (To make note of the torment I endured wondering if I *had* a voice audible to a man is superfluous. Suffice to say, it is a common enough experience in the presence of the great.)

Sartre did not believe that I was a flea. He stubbornly held to the belief that I was an American intellectual engrossed in the problem of finding himself. In his view I was only the voice of a body that had not yet materialized — an hypothesis that intrigued him greatly.

"Can a flea become a man?" I asked.

"Man," he said, "if you continue to refer to yourself as a flea, you'll wind up a flea. The trouble with you, the trouble with man, is that when he believed in God he felt like a flea and when he discontinued his belief he still felt like a flea. It's a habit not easy to rid oneself of.

"All I ask," he went on, "is that you refrain from calling yourself a flea and start calling yourself a man, no matter what limitations are bugging you." He smiled at his pun, and pleasantly surprised by it, indulged me by participating in what he believed was my delusion. "Once you become a man, Monsieur Flea, you must do all the things you left to God to do and you must explain all the things you let God get by without explaining."

Ah, what a glorious future I foresaw for myself as a man. I was to swallow God!

At that moment I almost swallowed Sartre, without another word exchanged, but something held me back. He had already coped with his existence and worked out for himself a *raison d'être*. Some young man, instead, who might take it from where Sartre left off. I could not deny myself the joys and anguish of my own development after I became a human being.

He crossed his legs, and since I happened to be sitting on his knee (without his knowledge), I found myself trapped between two knees in old tweed smelling of anisette and ink. When I finally struggled free he was inviting me out to meet a few of his friends.

Suffice to say, they considered me quite a phenomenon: a voice without a body. Nobody accepted the fact that I was a flea, a refusal that gave me considerable pain. Although I insisted that I was only a flea, my pride did not wholly concur in the *only*: a flea is more than they thought. But I did not nurse my grievance long. It may have been the heady fragrance of the wine combined with the conversation in which I figured as a human being among human beings, it may have been my potential astir — in any case, I found myself oddly susceptible to the charms of a particular woman.

Her name was Yvette. For a moment I had an almost irresistible urge to swallow her. But my reason told me, and my heart, that this was not what I really wanted since it would deprive me of her company, the company of the other. The fusion I wanted to achieve with her was of another kind.

She was a short, voluptuous woman with ivory skin, and I understood at once the feeling of the human male in regard to the female: with her help I could be more a man than I could be alone. I almost went out of my mind with despair at not having swallowed already somebody she would love.

That night, nestled down under the epaulet of her raincoat,

I accompanied her to her small studio in Montrouge. (She painted.) She was morose that night and had refused as escort one of the young men at the party, so luckily I was able to reveal my presence the moment she locked the door. As soon as I said, "Forgive me, but I came along," I was stricken with the fear she might order me out and, uncertain whether I had gone, sit all night in her clothes.

But strange to say she was the only one who had really believed I was a flea. For the first time that night I heard her laugh. "Forgive *me!*" she said. "But it is time for me to sleep. You may stay if you don't hop around in my bed." My heart both sang and sank. Then, humiliation on humiliation, she sat for half an hour without a stitch on, reading Heidegger. I was desperate to make myself substantial to that woman!

For three days I stayed with her in this frustrating relationship. On the fourth, she brought home a thin-nosed, smug and emaciated fellow from Chicago who was studying Medieval History at the Sorbonne. Since he carried a small suitcase in each hand, I judged he had come to stay. All night I stayed awake under the rug, sick with desire and jealousy. I could, I realized, have swallowed the young man beside her, but I disliked the fellow and my soul revolted against my becoming him. Towards morning, while they slept at last, a great homesickness overcame me — a longing not for place but for person. I yearned to return to the pad of my birth and there swallow the young man, who now appeared in my mind's eye with a singular luminosity. Enough time had been wasted as a parasitical *persona non grata* on this body and that, enough time under rugs.

By dog and man, it took me five days to get out to Orly airport. Once on the plane, I settled in with an American importer on his way to San Francisco. By week's end, I was back in the room of my origin. Everything was the same. My brother, the cat, was not in at the moment, but I saw that he still resided there: his chipped bowl, in which lay an unsavory lump of lamb's kidney, was out in the middle of the floor. I thought of him with both gratitude for his daring and disgust for his not daring enough.

My young man was seated at his table, huddled over pen and paper. The table was loaded with volumes — everybody who had ever commented on the condition of man was represented — and, as was like him, he had neglected to clear enough room for his own elbows. If I swallowed him, I mused charitably, whatever insect characteristics he might acquire would be no more obvious or disabling than those of other young men. Some had eyebrows like antennae; others had round bodies with small hands like insect feet; some stared out from behind glasses that resembled the great fixed eyes of a fly. As I regarded him from a pile of books at his right hand, he seemed the most appetizing thing I had ever seen. So, weary unto death of my existence as a flea, I swallowed him where he sat.

The Vault

HE HAD BOUGHT a conical, brasscolor metal lamp that clamped to the back of a chair by his wall bed and was adjustable, slanting its beam at the angle he chose. The old standing lamp with its fringed, bile-green shade of armadillo shape he had carried down by elevator and left at the manager's door. The low knotty-pine bookcase that he had found in the basement and dragged out from under a pile of greasy rugs, whose gray, hellish padding was still stuck to their undersides, was filled with the books he had mailed out to himself, care of the main branch of the public library, the day before he left St. Louis: his own four novels; a few obscure novels that had appealed to him and that nobody else had ever heard of; and the rest classics. He seldom reread the classics, knowing that if he were to open one at random a sense of salvation would grasp his chin and lift his head above water when he preferred to remain unreminded that he was drowning; his own novels he never opened, the effect of their pages, read only by himself and a few indifferent and unknowable strangers, was too much like a recurrence of neuralgia; the other obscure novels had not affected him at second reading as strongly as at the first and why try a third time? So this collection that he had shipped on ahead from one city to another was left unread.

Every evening he read, instead, newspapers, circulars, periodicals, newsletters, solicitations from organizations, saving a few of the pleas for the kitchen table where he wrote, each week, a small, responsive check to the organization that appeared to be most poor and yet most viable, a choice not easy to make. All other material was shifted from the pile of the unread on one chair to the pile of the discarded on another chair, both chairs in the middle of the room and, when the bed was lowered from its niche, already alongside it. When the discard pile grew unmanageable, slipping its top papers down under the narrow arms of the chair to the rug, he tied it with string, once over and across, and carried it down to the refuse cans.

Undressing was a prolonged activity. Sometimes he sat down on the bed after his trousers were off and his shirt and sweater still on and picked up some appealing paper; at other times, with nothing off but one shoe or both shoes and both socks, he paused in his labor to read part of a circular he had already placed on the discard pile. When he was at last in bed he read until the heat that was left in the room by the oven in the kitchen and by the small electric heater near the foot of the bed slowly faded and the cold air took over the apartment.

Now, in the warmth that was left, he sat against his two

pillows, in his hands a brochure of the Mapes Collection of 20th Century Literary Memorabilia of the Magruder University Library. He was about to be shown just what the archivist and librarian, Lionel P. Ackerman, had collected for that not yet famous but growing famous fast university. Over the past three years he had received from Dr. Ackerman five letters requesting his manuscripts, journals, and personal correspondence for honored preservation in the library's vault. In his reply to the first request he had stated that he did not feel his work warranted preservation and Dr. Ackerman had responded by return mail, astonished and dismayed that he, Vincent Villalba, thought so little of his genius. Was he not aware of his reverential following? He wrote back that the only following he ever expected was a very small one at his funeral. In the days that followed this exchange of letters he found that he was stirred by the request, the first of its kind ever directed to him in his fifty years. He imagined a student seventy, eighty years hence, writing his dissertation on Minor Writers of the Twentieth Century in the United States. Someone might even select him from among the many as subject for a Guggenheim paper; certainly he was obscure enough. But even with these possibilities in mind he did not acquiesce.

Shortly after that first flattering plea there came an invitation to the opening of the library's new home. Since he had resided at that time halfway across the country from the site, working his way west from library to library, he had been unable to attend. Seven days of celebration! Dinners at the residences of the university's administrators; sherry parties; ceremonies for those who had already bequeathed untold sums and for those who would upon their death bequeath; and on the ultimate night a dinner at the home of the university's president honoring Dr. Lionel P. Ackerman, librarian.

At Christmastime, cards came, never failing, with Ackerman's signature: one year an etching of a revolving display case in the Mapes Memorabilia section, another year an etching of the whole facade of the library. More than once he had thought seriously of complying with Dr. Ackerman's insistent plea, but in the archives of his own mind lay the almost forgotten wish to acquire a modest sum for his manuscripts and letters. If he finished the novel that had lain for five years in the bureaus of his rented rooms and if it received some acclaim and if the acclaim roused belated interest in his four previous novels, then — who knows?

This thin brochure with its wan gold cover was not the thing to calm himself with at bedtime, but how could he know in advance what was to agitate him and how could he put down an agitating item once he had started it? He had to see who Dr. Ackerman had persuaded to give over their manuscripts that, before his cajolery, must have seemed like the skins of dead elephants, remnants of some insane labor. No names yet. The structure itself came first, its description within a frame of curlicued plants and marble vases: *The architecture of the Magruder University Library is modern baroque, granting an opulent atmosphere to the Mapes Collection, which occupies the entire third floor. Here the walls of the exhibition room are comprised of glass bricks whose pristine lucidity conspires to create a magical illusion wherein space plays with time.* Good! Good! *A display of donated material, chosen from the vault every two weeks, slowly revolves in a circular glass case that is lit by recessed lighting that throws a strong yet not harsh light on the valuable gifts on view, and it is assured that no donor will be overlooked. Each will have his or her own two-week display.*

Into the magnificent vaults of Yale and Harvard is flowing like a mighty river the source materials of the 18th and 19th Centuries. We therefore claim the 20th Century. In the vault of the Mapes

Collection of the Magruder University Library will be embalmed the best minds of our time. In this vault humidity is maintained at an optimum level to preserve the donated materials forever. Acid-free envelopes will contain the journals, manuscripts, and other memorabilia of writers, poets, actors, politicians, soldiers, and critics.

Admit it, Villalba. It would be pleasant to lie acidless forever. He who had been troubled for so many years by acidity of the stomach and spirit — what more could he ask for than to lie free of the stuff forever? Dr. Ackerman was a God of Mercy. Yes, if he weren't a novelist also but altogether a librarian, he would like to be Dr. Ackerman.

The apartment was cooling off fast. A fog had come in over the city around noon, an immense and clammy catastrophe obliterating a hot, bright morning. That's the way it was in this city; he had been told about its changeable weather by friends in the East who had resided here. They had warned him never to expect a steady rise but always a sudden fall. Down in the street a couple drunks were quarreling, a man and a woman. They were entrenched down there, perhaps sitting on the curb, their voices rising up against the brick walls of the entire block and into his fourth-floor window. They could sit in the fog indefinitely, their minds on something else, because drunks were immune to cold. He, however, up here and out of the fog, was not immune. He was not clothed warmly enough to continue his reading and was too impressed with it to give it up. He got out of bed and from the closet took his bathrobe, a faded flannel garment once the elegant color of chamois, given him by his girlfriend fifteen years ago and worn down now with a hole in the seat the size of a hand. He wrapped the robe around his frail, slight self, tied the belt, climbed back into bed, and picked up the brochure where it lay, open and down, on the blanket. A giant photo of a rural route mailbox with its metal flag up, and on the box, in large, paint-dripping letters, the name BAUM. *Nothing deters Dr. Ackerman in his pursuit of memorabilia. Cross-country treks are not uncommon in his life. One such trek was to New Hampshire* — Wasn't that two states away from the library? — *to the turkey farm of Philip Baum, who, after the critical failure of his only novel,* A Time of Silence, *now a classic, retired in bitterness to raise turkeys for the Thanksgiving market. His mailbox was transported back by Dr. Ackerman to become a permanent part of the Mapes Collection.*

He felt for his nightcap under his pillows and spread it down over his bald head to his eyebrows. It was soft, thin, cut from a woman's cotton stocking and possibly the only one in America. Would Ackerman be pleased to receive it? Everybody had a mailbox but nobody wore a nightcap though the loss of hair among the male population was on the increase or hair was on the decrease — whichever way Ackerman would choose to word it. He never wore it when there was company in bed with him and so it might be the most personal souvenir that Ackerman would ever get.

Photos of typescript pages from novels whose titles rang distant and discordant bells, *Prince Cockspur, Over the Edge*. There was only a bare minimum of interlinear changes but to Dr. Ackerman they must have appeared significant, an insight into the mysteries of the creative mind. To Villalba the pages were the faces of the authors, clean, respectable, free of doubt, the nose hairs and the ear hairs trimmed. Somebody's pen! Of course! An item to be expected, its picture superimposed on a manuscript page. A desk pen, its socket set in a jagged hunk of marble. Arnold Carewe's was the hand that had imbued this pen with a sense of existence that distinguished it from all other similar pens on the desks of the nation's insurance agents. Its rather fattish owner had collapsed from a heart attack a year ago, but every twenty-five years or so into eternity that pen would go round and round in the display case, erect, slender, virile. A nightcap spoke of sloth, baldness, hypochondria, aloneness. It was also an anachronism. A man would have to be a great one, nothing less than Tolstoy, to overcome a nightcap in a display case.

Across from the Carewe mementos was another typescript page, this one from *The Judges* by Kurt Hanson. The novel was among the obscure ones in his knotty-pine bookcase, the ones he could not persuade himself to sell to a high-class used bookstore or even to give away to friends. So, after all, Ackerman had a few prizes, even Hanson's suicide note, superimposed on the lower right corner of the manuscript page, hardly legible, and, once figured out, completely lacking the originality of his novel — *Can't take it anymore*. Below the pictures, Ackerman's mortician's pity: *Kurt Hanson took his life by hanging in tragic reaction to the unfavorable criticism of his novel, that thirty-seven years later was to be declared a classic by the dean of critics, Irwin Unwin who, browsing in a used book store in upper New York state without his glasses, purchased the book mistakenly assuming it was an early and neglected work of the great novelist Knut Hamsun. Upon reading it he proclaimed it an American milestone.*

His hand turned the page calmly as if it were not helpless but in control. Nothing, no periodical or daily paper or one-shot brochure, was complete without a cartoon. *The comic strip, so dear to the hearts of so many generations of Americans, is amply represented by a forty-one-year collection of the longest enduring of these, "Lil Gurlilocks," and by original drawings from twenty-seven others.* Eight strips stretched across a double spread, one of Willy Nilly, a midget recruit, running to get in the chow line; one of Hound Dog Dudley, an unkempt giant of a boy, beating a city slicker with a large tree limb; the others he bypassed. What if he had complied and sent in his papers? Would they lie forever between Willy Nilly and Lil Gurlilocks, as midgety as the one, as blank-eyed as the other? If he were ever to consent he would specify that his resting-place be next to that of Kurt Hanson, whose yearnings to crumble and disintegrate and escape the company of his vault mates must be an awesome, invisible plea between those lines that he had written when alive. No. On second thought, not even for Hanson's sake, not even to comfort that compadre, would he consent to spend the rest of eternity in the company of Cockspur and Willy Nilly.

The pages that were now before him, his palm spreading flat the center of the brochure, presented him with still another manuscript. *In the confident belief that the science fiction genre represents the future not only in its depiction of life to come but in the concepts it dares to create in the realm of literature, Dr. Ackerman has sought out the famous of the genre to preserve for, and perhaps amaze with their prophetic sense, the readers of the centuries ahead. The page above is from the novel* Remarkable Rover *by Jacob R. Kaltwasser, physicist, novelist, screenwriter, the engrossing story of a food cell, anthropomorphized, to be sure, but altogether credible, and his transformative stages in the body of a beautiful young woman.* Since he had always been ashamed of his resistance to science fiction, at a loss whenever some library patron accosted him to ask if he had read the latest one, now at last he gave in, persuaded by Dr. Ackerman's prophecy. The pictured page was 36: "*. . . what enzymes I must come to grips with first. In that way I will know how much of me is to disappear.*"

"*Let's not use that word disappear,*" said Dr. Ryerson.

"*I'm only facing facts,*" said Garry.

"*There are different ways of facing facts,*" said the doctor. "*If you call the process . . .*"

"*Assimilation?*" cut in Garry.

"*Don't interrupt. You are altogether too fearful of the changes*

awaiting you." Who was Doctor Ryerson? That was the trouble
with starting a novel in the middle. Was he another food particle
or was he a miniatured human being who had come along as a
spiritual advisor? *"Call it,"* Dr. Ryerson said, *"transcendence."*

*Suddenly an acrid-smelling avalanche poured down on them.
"What is it?" cried Garry, attempting to escape. Instead, to his dis-
may he found he was inundated. It was worse than the experience
in Denise's mouth. He had managed to avoid too much damage by
her teeth, but there was no avoiding this deluge.*

*"It's hydrochloric acid!" cried Dr. Ryerson, riding the waves in his
transparent bathosphere suit.*

Villalba closed the brochure and leaned sideways to place it
on the pile of material whose contents had been explored. The
fog and wind of this city were aggravating his joints. At noon, on
the top floor of the library, pausing in his pursuit of information,
he had gazed out toward the north where the bay was located and
concealed from his sight by other buildings that were higher,
naturally, than the main branch of the public library. He had
watched the fog bank approach in a rush, observed its crest torn
off ceaselessly and all its edges disappearing, and now he knew
where they had gone, those tails and feelers of fog. They had slid
into his joints. He lay in the neon-tinged darkness with fog in his
joints and fearful of yet another assault: German measles was
going around. Four workers in the library were down with it and
three of the patrons, while chatting with him, had told him of
their bouts with the disease. If it began with aches in the joints,
as they had informed him, perhaps his aches were not a result of
the fog but symptomatic of the disease. Although he would get
rid of the pile on the discard chair tomorrow after work, the presence near his bed of the brochure weakened him for the assault
by the epidemic. Embalm. What a terrorizing word. Dr. Ackerman preferred his authors dead.

· Upstairs someone was padding around listening to a radio talk show. He heard the cheery hello of the host, and the fainter, somewhat nasal, slowly reasoning voice of the phoner-in. Then the host's blows of hard reason to the topic obsessing the drag man whose wavering, blundering voice fought on up to the final blow that cut the connection. Then the cheery hello again for the next drag. He lay on his back, gazing upward, unable to hear the distinct words, hearing only the repetitious patterns and their reverberations. Controversy in America, the haggling and haranguing over the point-beside-the-point, beat down through the ceiling, assaulting his spirit. Or had he a spirit? It was dissolved a long time ago in the hydrochloric acid bath of Dr. Ackerman's 20th Century. It had disappeared in the act of complying with all orders preceding its death and was nowhere around now to attempt any countermanding, any revolt. Some spirits survived, they did not disappear—dread word. They transcended themselves, as Garry, the food particle, surely would at the end of the novel. Not his, though. If he gave over to Dr. Ackerman his manuscripts and notes to be placed among the insignificant others, they would remain for an eternity unread, unexamined, unwondered about, as dead as the being who had jotted it all down. Nobody's finger running down the alphabetical list of authors in the Mapes Collection would stop at the name of Villalba. Obscure in his own era, he would remain obscure forever if he were to lie forever in the Mapes vault. Gone, unrecallable, unembalmed, obliterated, he would find some relief in obscurity.

A curse on Dr. Ackerman for keeping him awake. He reached up into the cold, switched on his lamp, sat up and pushed up the left sleeve of his pajamas. No spots anywhere along the arm. Rashes began on the belly or around the waist, everybody knew that. He pulled up the pajama shirt and examined his waist, pushed down the pants and examined his belly. If the spirit was gone the body was sure to follow upon discovering the loss of its inseparable companion. Dr. Ackerman's author lay in his fold-out bed, searching as fearfully for measle spots on his belly as for the fingerprints of death.

Return of the Griffins

GUNAR VRIES, emissary to the United Nations Conference in New York from the European Democracy of S———, sat on the edge of his bed in his hotel room, removing his shoes and socks.

He had declined to be present that evening at a party given in his honor by a wealthy expatriate, telephoning his regrets. In his stead he had sent his aide, a handsome young man who, besides being secretary and translator, was also a composer of symphonies, instructing him to confine himself to seduction and to the piano. As for Gunar Vries, he had had his supper sent up and after the tray was removed had locked his door and set himself to his writing: his daily personal letter to his president, in which he imparted observations too detailed to be made by phone, and letters to the members of his family, his wife Alice and his son Theodore at the Technological University. When he had signed his name for the third time, the night was late.

He was removing his second sock when the bed moved. He grasped the blankets to keep from being thrown, believing that an earthquake had struck. But the bottles did not slide from the dresser, no particles of ceiling fell, the chandelier did not sway. Only the bed moved. Then through his lifted knees he saw emerging from beneath the bed the head of an eagle, but three times the size of an eagle's head, and stretching out for a grip of the rug, an eagle's claw. Then followed a lion's body. So the lion had an eagle's head. Or the eagle had a lion's body.

When the creature emerged completely, Gunar saw that it had also two wings, great eagle wings, that now it stretched one at a time across the floor. The wing roots crackled, and the feathers swept across the rug with a swishing, rushing sound. The creature slouched to the center of the room, its forelegs lifting stiffly, like a bird's legs, but in coordination with its hindlegs, that moved in the indolently potent manner of a lion.

Still heavy with sleep, the monster fell over on its side and gently lifting its wing, turned its head under and with closed beak nuzzled along the feather pocket, in this way nudging itself to wakefulness and woe again. Then lifting its head, swinging it around and up, the creature looked straight at Gunar Vries. The eagle part took prominence — the curved beak, hard as stone, the thick encasing of golden feathers over its head, touched with red at the breast and extending down its forelegs to the very toes. Lion ears protruded through the feathers but were laid sleekly back. Its eyes burned ruby bright in the semi-darkness.

"Change of climate," it explained, "makes me sleepy."

Before he had entered politics, more than twenty years ago, Gunar Vries had been professor of ancient Greek civilization at the University of Afia, capital of S———. His past enabled him to recognize the creature. "Griffin?" he asked. "Is that your name?" He had several cats on his farm and a trained falcon, and spoke always with tenderness and respect to them, as now he spoke to this great creature.

"Yes," replied the griffin, "and of the pure strain. If you're wondering about the Sphinx and her woman's face, one of us became enamored of a virgin of your species; though I can't see what he saw in her."

The griffin spoke its own language, like no other in the world, and yet a concoction of them all, with archaic Greek like a warrior's chariot rumbling and shining through. It was like everything unspoken that a word cannot be put to and that is comprehended more readily than the spoken among men of different languages.

"You've been away several years," said Gunar, covering his bare feet again with shoes and socks. "What did you do in the time?"

"Took ourselves to the mountains of India," replied the griffin. "Sat in the sun, on the thresholds of our caves, or caught the Arimaspi, one-eyed men who seek gold in the mountains, ate them in a shrugging fashion, already gorged with our prowess. I might ask the same question of you. What didn't you do? By Apollo! Procreated not individuals but nations. Took the lid off a water kettle, and what steams out but ships and cities. Times have changed."

The creature's breath began to fill the room, an overly warm breath, smelling of raw meat, the rich, dark, stinging smell of blood clots and liver.

Gunar Vries had his trousers on and his gray hunting shirt that he wore evenings by himself, but he was cold. He turned the radiator higher. "I presume," he said, standing with his back to the heat, "that you wandered down alone?"

"Only one of the vanguard," replied the creature, preening its breast.

Now Gunar Vries was fully aware of the monsters' significance. They were in their time sacred to Apollo, whose chariot they drew, and as Apollo was the prophetical deity, whose oracle when consulted delivered itself in enigmas, the word griffin, too, meant enigma. And because he was fully aware of this, he preferred not to seem aware.

The emissary rubbed his hands together briskly to make them warm. "What's the occasion?" he inquired.

The feigned innocence did not escape the griffin. The creature picked it apart like picking the tortoise from the shell. A hissing contempt came from its nostrils and partially opened beak. For a moment there seemed to be a geyser in the room.

"Emissary to the UN," it replied, "a conference called to promote the flowering of humanity, and all the time the delegates hard put to it to breathe with the possibility of atomic dust in the air no more than five years from now. And you want to know the occasion! Can you think of a time when the world faced a greater enigma?"

Gunar Vries was indeed concerned for humanity. It was something he traveled with in addition to his aide and his portfolio. Yet now it seemed to him that it was humanity in the abstract he had been carrying around—the formalities, the rules and regulations, the paperwork of a conference, humanity carefully composed and delivered with dignity. At the griffin's words, humanity suddenly became a third party in the room, and Gunar shivered with life, he shook convulsively as children do in excitement.

The monster slunk around the room, which became small as the cage in which a circus lion is confined. When it came to the desk it turned its head with ponderous grace and ran its eyes over the letters. Gunar Vries stirred indignantly and stepped forward, but on second thought was stricken with shame for his disrespect and stopped still. The griffin turned away, but in the turning managed to drop the nictitating membrane of its eyes, and the perusal became an act of idle curiosity. It padded away languidly, disdainfully, dragging one wing, and the emissary, hearing a strange clicking noise along the floor, looked down and saw for the first time the full length of the creature's talons. At each step they were nicking small holes in the rug.

The creature sat down by the window, and the tasseled end of its tail lifted and fell. There was a feminine restlessness in the way its feathers quivered, and at the same time a great seething of male energy that propelled it forward even as it sat still. "Lift the window for me," it said, "and let me out on the ledge. Isn't there a park across the street?"

The emissary drew up the venetian blind and opened the window. The night entered, cold and fragrant with grass. The lamps in the park were almost pure white, as if encrusted with snow, and shone up through the delicate branches of the trees. People were sitting on the benches, talking and glancing up at the lighted windows of the hotel, where many dignitaries were in residence. Newsboys had built a fire in a refuse can, and taximen and journalists, tired of the plush and statuary of the lobby, were warming their hands around it. An ornate ledge ran along beneath the windows of the top floor, and the griffin leaped onto this.

"It won't be harmed," Gunar Vries told himself. "It's too fabulous. Even an oaf can see." A look of being protected lay in its eyes, a true and natural hauteur from an ancient epoch. He closed the window, and in his mind's eye he saw the creature continuing swiftly along the ledge, tail and wings spread out a bit, a dark and slithering form against the faintly lighted sky.

He went to his desk, took up his pen, and wrote in postscript on the letter to his president, *"My dear friend: This evening I saw one of the first griffins to return. Their coming, though unpredictable, was nevertheless inevitable. They will remain, I gather, until we decide our fate, one way or another."* Hearing a strange cry in the night, a mingling of lion's roar and eagle's scream and more than both, he wrote further, *"The cry of the griffin in the great cities of the world will become as familiar as the cry of the cock in the country, and even as the cock's cry wakens us from sleep and is portentous of the morning when we shall not be alive to hear it, so the cry of the griffin, on the roofs above traffic, is troublous, calling us, humanity, to a cognizance of our existence and heralding our possible end."*

WHEN GUNAR awoke in the morning it was, as every day, to no other thought but the Conference. Not until he passed the desk on his return from his bath and saw that the three letters had been taken up by his aide for mailing was he reminded of the griffin. He stood still, startled and amused by such a dream. Well, the times evoked it. He had never before worked under such a strain, and the enigma of the times had taken form and substance, emerged in his dream a thing in itself, had become a living creature.

But as he was dressing, the laughter within ceased, and he was overcome by melancholy. It came to him that the griffin might have been other than a dream. His few hours of sleep had been shallow and hot, as if he had slept in a thunderstorm; remembering his sleep, he was almost certain he had not dreamed. If the fabulous being had appeared, it had been an actual one. *But, of course, it had not appeared.* He could negate the event, he could prove it had been a dream by seeing again his letter to his president, the signature constituting the end, without postscript. He walked slowly to the door of the adjoining apartment, already tired as if at the end of the day. How old was he now? Fifty-six? And how long did men live, usually?

"Norbert, young man," he called, rapping at the half-open door, "you've not posted the letters yet? The three letters?"

His aide appeared at the door, opening it wider. "They made the plane at seven-thirty."

"The letter to the president?"

"All three were sealed," said Norbert, "and envelopes addressed. Did you wish to make changes?"

"A whim," he replied. He looked sharply at his aide. Norbert wrote symphonies, the modern kind; his disharmonies were not what they seemed but merged into a complete harmony. Was he not the one to understand the griffin? "If I tell him," thought Gunar, "if I tell him, laughing a little, with gestures, with shudders, why, two believing will make it untrue."

But Norbert seemed more erect than usual this morning, his eyes bluer, his fair hair fairer. He liked parties, and the atmosphere for him was still charged with his virtuosity. The emissary decided that to explain the griffin to him would bring the creature down to the level of a piano recital and the sensual laughter of bare-armed women.

"Come," he said, signaling for Norbert to accompany him.

In the cab Gunar sat in a corner, holding his hat and gloves on his crossed knees, listening to Norbert read foreign newspapers on the UN proceedings. The cab came to a halt as traffic changed, and he gazed into the street. In a basement tailor shop, the name on the window so worn that the dim light within turned the letters translucent and coppery, a tailor sat sewing at his machine while his wife sat by the window, drinking from a cup.

As Gunar took in the shop and its occupants, he saw his second griffin. She — it was a female, as he could tell by the lack of red feathers on her breast — was sliding along the fence before the row of basement shops, the eagle head lifted and stiff with impending alarm.

He grasped Norbert's hand, and the young man laid down his paper. "You see," he said, as if he had tried before to convince his aide, "a female griffin."

Norbert bent across him to look. The griffin slipped down the stairs into the tailor's shop, pushing the door open with a claw, and for a moment Gunar saw, simultaneously, the eagle's head through the window and the lion's tail waving on the stairs. Persons passing paid no attention, or only slight, as to a cat or a sparrow. The couple did not look up, neither the man from his sewing nor the wife from her cup. Gunar Vries was appalled. They went about their pursuits as before, while this enigma, this beast of life or death, slid along their streets, jangled their business bells.

"But are they so common a sight already?" he asked.

"What are?" Norbert had taken up his reading again, but courteously allowed himself to be engaged in conversation.

"The griffins. A female went into the tailor shop and you made no to-do about it."

"I didn't see one," said Norbert. "I didn't know what to look for. I'm sorry. What is it like?"

Gunar Vries drew into his corner again. "It's not a thing that you look for," he replied.

The delegates to the General Assembly of the United Nations assembled at their headquarters. Gunar Vries sat in his place, his aide beside him, taking no part in the conversation before the fall of the gavel. The chairman entered, and following at his heels was a male griffin, larger, older than the one that had slept in Gunar's room. The creature was hoary and unkempt. Its eyes were yellow fire. It seated itself to the right of the chairman and with archaic grace surveyed the persons assembled.

THAT EVENING after supper the president replied by telephone. "Gunar, what's this talk of a griffin?" he asked. "It's a beast of classical antiquity, is it not? Well, to what use are you putting it?"

Ernest Gorgas was a fine man, and there was no one Gunar respected more. But how impotent the president's voice, how distant not only in space but in time! Gunar had the peculiar anticipatory feeling of hearing it fade away, as if mankind were running instantly into a post-historic age.

"Gunar," the president continued, his voice grinding into the receiver, louder, adamant, yet deeply kind and respectful, "the plea that you made to the Assembly today for international unity was the most moving I have ever heard. And the delivery of it — the eloquence, the impassioned tone! Maneuvering it the way you did was uncalled for and yet the most called-for thing in the world. If you are in your way sidestepping praise, being modest, bringing up this tale of a griffin coming to your room with a warning, it's no use. Gunar, my friend, there is no appointment that I have made in my term of office that has given me greater satisfaction."

"Ernest," replied Gunar, "the man who feels that he is not deserving of praise makes no move to sidestep it. He has a deaf place in his ear the size of a pea, and with this he hears praise. No, my friend, a male griffin *was* in my room last evening. Since then I have seen two more. One, slipping along the street, female and playing nervous; the other, a more bestial creature and at the same time looking as if imbued with an omniscient intelligence.

It was sitting to the right of the chairman today and commented often, succinctly, too. But though its voice was louder than any there it went unheard. At the conclusion of my speech it came to me and told me that it had heard Demosthenes, and that my eloquence exceeded his. It had been sent alone to take in the American Revolution and had heard Patrick Henry — it said that that gentleman's vigor did not touch mine. I did not take these comparisons as praise but was convinced that the precariousness of our times has never been equalled and that orators are made by the periods in which they live."

A long pause followed. When the president spoke again the subject was changed. He inquired about the discussions under way, Gunar's criticism and forecast of results.

Within another day the rumor had been circulated among the delegates that Gunar Vries, emissary from S———, was suffering from hallucinations. The suspicion was not relayed to newsmen or to anyone outside the circle of official delegates. It was a matter of respect not only for the member, as a distinguished person, and for his family, but for the delegates combined. If one was susceptible to weakness of this kind, it might be construed that all were. The curious thing was that the emissary seemed to be in full command of his intelligence while at the Conference table. No criticism could be cast upon the deft, perspicacious way in which he handled his country's interest. Not only this, he was one of the most energetic in tackling the problems of all humanity.

GUNAR VRIES was called home on the second day after his speech. Newsmen, inquiring of him the reason for his departure, were told that he believed that his president was in possession of information that could not be discussed by phone or letter or through a messenger. In Gunar's place, to be guided by Norbert through the formalities, there appeared the youngest member of the supreme court of S———, a man not much older than Norbert, but with his own history up to ninety years already in his eyes.

Carrying his portfolio, Gunar Vries returned to S———. He was met at the airport by the president, and together they were driven to the palace. They dined and secluded themselves in the president's study.

"Gunar," said Ernest, as they sat facing each other, "I could not ask for a better emissary. You have used the energy of twelve men. Now, wound up as you are, you will think I am crazy, you will think I am reckless putting your personal health before the welfare of the nation. But I want you to take a rest for a while. Let someone else, not of your caliber but competent enough, assume your duties. You go to your farm, wear an old hat, go hunting, milk your cows, sow your wheat. We need as many hands as we can get working the land, and as much space yielding. Go home for a while, Gunar."

Gunar Vries had never been so frightened in his life. It was like the fear, only worse, that he had experienced as a boy of seventeen, when he had left his father and come to the city to study, when for the first time he had lived alone. For several days he had been almost unable to breathe. He had thought he would never again see his father or make a friend, he had thought that he was trapped in that one room forever.

"Has any action of mine," Gunar now asked slowly, "met with your disapproval? Have you found that the ability I evidenced as your minister of foreign affairs, have you found that this ability falls short of my responsibility as a delegate to the United Nations?"

Ernest gripped his forehead, half-hid his painful eyes with his hand. "They say that you see griffins."

"But I told you so myself."

"Doesn't it seem peculiar to you?"

"You prefer to quote the ones to whom it seems peculiar? No, my friend, it is the most natural thing in the world."

"But you are the only one who sees them."

"Does that fact make the griffin non-existent?" He felt a sharp derision coming on, took out his handkerchief and blew his nose. He tried to suppress the snort, but could not. It was his opinion of organized disorganization.

"If you take such a derogatory view of the Conference," the president said, "you won't want to return."

"On the contrary," Gunar replied, leaning forward to stuff his handkerchief away in his rear pocket. "They need me. They can't do without me. The time will come, believe me, when everyone there will see that creature sitting to the right of the chairman. And what a creature! What a magnificent creature!"

"Gunar." The president hesitated. "Before you go home, perhaps it would be wise for you to consult a psychiatrist. They have not all gone to greener pastures in the United States. There might be still a capable one or two practicing in France or Switzerland."

"I would have no belief in him if he did not see griffins himself," replied Gunar, laughing a little. "But for your sake, to relieve you of anxiety and shame, I shall resign from the UN and from the Ministry. Name someone else to the post."

He wanted to rise from the chair, as a gesture fitting to climax, but found that he could not. His heart was palpitating. Well, he had seen his father again, made a friend, and been in so many rooms he could not remember them all. A boy's loneliness doesn't last, nor does that of a disgraced diplomat. You reach out for people, you have no more enemies. . . .

GUNAR TRAVELED home by train that night, and a female griffin was co-occupant of his compartment. When he entered, she was already asleep on the couch, eagle head tucked under her right wing, left wing and left hindleg hanging to the floor. He sat opposite her and watched her in the dimly lit, rocking compartment.

He rode to his farm on the wagon of a neighbor. "You want to surprise Mrs. Vries?" the neighbor asked. The man had found Gunar, portfolio in hand, standing by his wagon, waiting for him to come from the assessor's office.

"No," replied Gunar. "I just came home, that's all."

"You are tired from the Conference?" the neighbor inquired, believing that it was over. He noticed the diplomat's sagging shoulders and sadness, and he halted the horses. "What's the world coming to?" he asked, gently, confidentially, as if Gunar Vries was the one to know.

And Gunar Vries laid his brow in his hand and wept, while the morning sun got in under his overcoat collar and warmed the nape of his neck.

For several days he went about his farm like a man taking a rest. He milked the cows, drove the tractor. There was a deep, still pool in his forest and he went to bathe in it, likening it to his loneliness. If he were drowning in it and cried out, no man would be near enough to help him. But when he left the pool and dressed again, his body was clean and deserving of respect because of its contact with loneliness, and approaching the farm he loved instantly from afar every small figure working.

Then one morning he saw on the roof of the east barn a young male griffin, and he called to it. The creature turned its large golden head slantwise.

"Come," coaxed Gunar, "a lamb? A pan of milk?" And when the creature eyed him without replying, he added, "A calf?"

The griffin dropped its beak and picked at something between its toes. "But I ate, just a couple of centuries ago. Caught four Arimaspi in a ravine."

ALICE BEGGED Gunar to wait until she summoned Theodore, but he said no, that he would probably meet the boy in the city.

"Ah!" he exclaimed, for she had given him an idea. "I intend to speak on the steps of the Technological University anyway. When the scientific students see my griffin, it will be a triumph, believe me."

She went along the road with him, holding his elbow against her side and crying, and he bent his head away, unable to bear her grimaces. The griffin was slinking along the other side of the fence, and in a fit of energy suddenly both flew and ran, beating its wings close to earth, for a good half-mile down the fence. Why couldn't she see a thing like that?

He halted and caressed her, pushing back her short, pale hair. "Do you know that I love you?" he asked.

"Yes," she wept.

"The tour is a minor thing," he said. "I make it simply to return to you. If I don't go, how much longer and of what consequence will our love be?"

WHEN HE SET out again, alone, the griffin was returning to meet him, loping.

So he came into Afia, capital of S———, with the griffin at his side. He was dressed as for a session of the UN. He wore his favorite suit, tailored in London of a fine Scottish tweed, a white shirt, a dark red silk tie, and he carried a black Homberg and gray suede gloves. He took rooms in a first-rate hotel.

Entering the park around which were grouped the government buildings, he mounted the flagpole base and pleaded with refugees, messengers passing to and fro, and clerks eating their lunches, to recognize his companion. In the evening he let himself be enveloped by the crowds pouring into the operas and symphonies and cinemas. Jostled and stepped upon, he began to recount his experiences, and some persons, with mail order tickets and in no hurry, tarried around him. At midnight, when the streets were being deserted, he returned to his hotel, and the griffin spent the night in the vicinity.

By the second day word had circulated that this man in the streets was actually Gunar Vries, come to tell of the existence of a fabulous beast or bird. The citizens jammed the streets, the fire-escapes, the roofs for blocks around the House of Commerce, and Gunar made his speech on the steps facing the park. Overjoyed as he was with the size of his audience, he spoke with such passion that the griffin, already unnerved by the crowd, its flesh creeping with the emissary's harping upon its existence, suddenly rose straight up into the air, screaming.

"Can't you see it?" Gunar Vries cried, pointing to the griffin beating the air, its beak open and its tongue flickering, its eyes fierier than ever, absorbing the three o'clock sun. After hovering thirty feet above Gunar's head, it continued up and settled on a cornice three stories above him.

The people gazed upward, but lowered their eyes with no change in them. They did not ridicule the speaker, however. They were solemn and attentive, remembering the man he once was. While about them, more griffins, curious as to the throngs, flew in and came to rest on the roofs of distant buildings, their dark forms like statues of themselves against the sky.

Gunar Vries descended the steps, and the people made way for him. He was not disheartened. There was time for other cities and other assemblages. He wanted especially to draw a great crowd in New York, city of the Conference. The griffin flew down and followed at his heels; he heard its wings flapping in descent and then the click of its claws on the stone. A guttural warble was in its throat, a sign of uneasiness.

Two members of the police force stepped through the crowd to Gunar Vries. The force had been reluctant to take action against him for disturbing the peace, considering his prestige, but during the course of his speech they had received instructions from Ernest Gorgas himself: "Quietly, with respect for his person as a private citizen and as a former diplomat, arrest and transport him to quarters in the Hall of Justice. Detain him there until further instructions."

"Gunar Vries," said one, "it's the president's wish."

"If I resist?" he asked.

The other officer touched his elbow, and Gunar told himself, "All their force will be unavailing and will seem afterward like a touch at my elbow." He reached behind him, laid his hand on the griffin, and brought it forward.

"If I mount you," he asked, "can you rise with my weight?"

The griffin nodded, but was perturbed and glazed its eyes. "When you asked me to accompany you, did you also ask that I convey you? It's seldom we convey a mortal."

"That's what it's come to," said Gunar.

The griffin rose reluctantly in the stance of a lion rampant, but the emissary, stepping forward to place his arms around the eagle's neck and seat himself upon the lion's rump, was detained by the officers, who came in under the wing, each taking an elbow and an armpit, and prevailing against him.

Gunar Vries was deposited in the cell reserved for politicians, bankers, celebrated attorneys, actresses, professors. Here were ashtrays, a watercooler and dispenser. The furniture, though old and sagging, was still substantial, with faintly yellowed cro-

cheted stars on the chairbacks. Waiting for him were his attorney
and a psychiatrist, a jovial, plump young man.

"If they want bail," said Gunar to his attorney, "then give it to
them. I'll be out of the country by morning."

"They're afraid of that," his attorney replied, a man competent
as he was handsome. "How would it look, Gunar," he chided, "for
a man of your status to misrepresent the country? The other
nations will say, 'What choice was this?' They'll have respect for
no emissary from S———."

The doctor, with whom he had shaken hands and who had
been listening, kindly, alertly, smoking a cigarette, now spoke
up. "Mr. Vries, contrary to the expressed wishes of Mr. Ernest
Gorgas, I am not going to ask your participation in any analysis. I
want a few answers from yourself to clarify, not my point of view
as a doctor, but your own, as a man of responsibility. You claim to
see griffins, beasts of ancient mythology. Is that true?"

"True," replied Gunar, "both that I claim to and that I see
them." He took a cigarette from the silver case the doctor prof-
fered him.

"And why griffins?" asked the doctor.

"Why not?" replied Gunar. "Because that's what they are.
They're not snakes, they're not elephants. I'm sorry. I cannot
make it as simple as that."

"No, no!" laughed the doctor, lighting Gunar's cigarette. His
hand shook, and his small eyes, small mouth, and small mus-
tache all laughed in his round face. "Why have they returned, I
mean. Are they, to you, explanatory of our time?"

Well, here was a man after Gunar's own heart, and he would
forget, in his appreciation, any ulterior motive the man might
have of undermining that which he so eagerly explained.

And so he told of the creature's history and the meaning of its name, and the doctor was absorbed and nodded his head. "Tell me of a time," said Gunar, "when the world faced a greater enigma. We'll either make the earth fruitful as it has never been or we'll exterminate ourselves. We'll either wipe out everything we've built upon, all past epochs, or we'll go on to a greater time than man has ever known. If you look at the situation with your eyes open you'll find that it's quite a creature, a thing with eagle wings and the body of a lion and with eyes of fire."

Gunar ceased, having heard the flapping of wings outside the window as the griffin ascended to the roof. It had followed him, as he had expected.

"Well, it's a pity," sighed the doctor, "that only one man sees them."

The attorney bent forward impatiently. "The president is aware that as a private citizen you may speak as you wish. Nevertheless, he would like your promise, as the promise of a dear friend, that you will make no further speeches in public or in private assembly calling upon the people to recognize the existence of these creatures."

"You tell Ernest," replied Gunar, "that they're bigger than he is."

"Will you commit him?" the attorney asked the doctor.

The doctor had risen, as if he had no more to ask. He shook his head, pressed out his cigarette in the tray. "I prefer," he said, "to commit those persons who cannot see them."

The two men left him to consult by telephone with the president. When they returned they brought with them the guard, as obliging to authority in release of the emissary as in confinement of him.

Gunar Vries picked up his hat and gloves. "There is one on the roof now," he said to the doctor, "if you care to see it."

This was an old prison, rigged up now with electricity and hot water. They went up the circular stone staircase, and the guard unlocked the gate. The griffin was lying on the parapet, drooping over the edge to watch the traffic three stories below, and at times lifting its head to look at the pigeons cooing and bobbing, circling and fluttering. It was large and dark against the pale yellow haze of the setting sun, and its feathers were delicately ruffled.

"Doctor," said Gunar, "do not let me lose faith in you."

"I see it," the doctor assured him.

The attorney coughed in vicarious embarrassment.

Gunar stepped to the parapet, the doctor and attorney following. "Can we try our flight again?" he asked the griffin. The doctor turned pale, and Gunar, watching for just this response, continued, "Its back is broad enough and its neck the right size for my arms. I'll hamper it a bit, perhaps, but we'll manage. You think now that it's not here at all for me to climb upon, but an idea came to me while I was trying to mount it in the park: If I am afraid, then I am not certain of the griffin myself. In this way, by trusting myself to it, I prove its existence."

The doctor was plunged into remorse and self-doubt. He stood stock-still, his arms hanging numbly at his sides.

Suddenly the attorney was cognizant of Gunar Vries' kindliness, of depths to the man he had not considered. He placed his hand on Gunar's arm. "Gunar," he implored him, "we shall provide you with first-class accommodation by whatever means you care to travel. I shall see to it myself. I shall speak to the president and to the Chamber of Representatives. You will be authorized to go — indeed, dispatched."

But Gunar Vries had hold of the griffin's rear leg and drew himself onto the parapet. The guard, having taken the respite to smoke a cigarette, was leaning against the gate, watching the men, believing that anything was sanctioned. And Gunar Vries, knowing that in a moment the three men would toss off their stupefaction and converge upon him, threw himself upon the griffin.

THEY FLEW in a westerly direction, passing over the city. The night moved up from behind and overtook them. With the earth so far below them, Gunar was not sure whether they were still over Europe or had reached the Atlantic Ocean.

"Can you drop a bit closer to earth?" Gunar called forward, and his voice was not as he expected it to be, bounced or pummeled by the wind, but went out into calm air, the atmosphere into which an oracle speaks.

"What for?" the griffin asked.

"But can you see any lights?"

The griffin glanced sideways in derision, enabling Gunar to see its eye, which was a blue distilled from the night, like a pure blue flame, and in it were reflected, nebulously, the lights of a city he believed to be New York.

fragment

of a novel

The Flood Again

HE CALLED ME by the name he said suited me, he never called
me by my real name. I knew *his* name, of course. There was no
way I could not know his name, but I never called him by that
name. And I never told anyone about him. When it began, only
my brother knew, and Josie, my closest friend, knew. The other
day a biography came out, and the man who wrote it gave the
impression of knowing everything about him, but he didn't know
anything about me, though so much about my life was common
knowledge. There was mention of a mistress, some other important man's ex-wife, who was happy to tell all, but what went on
between them lasted only a year or so. As for us, we met every

summer for three years, and, after that, whenever we could, and he kept in touch with me for a long time, and nobody knew, not even his closest colleagues, who seemed to know all the inviolable secrets of every country in the world.

The men who came every summer to that place he scoffingly called the Sacred Grove belonged to the upper reaches of government and industry, and you could see who they were on the nights some came out from that encampment to spend an hour or so with the women waiting for them in the hotels and bars along the river. About those men — you recognized one or two of the very important ones, you'd seen them on the TV newscasts, but for the rest you didn't really know who they were except that they were important enough and some fabulously rich enough to get their invitations to the summer doings. He was one of those who were always invited and whose presence enhanced that exclusivity.

The first time I went out to that little town on the Russian River I was just twenty. I went there with Josie on a day off from our waitress jobs. We went in her old convertible, driving north from San Francisco along the ocean and through the forest. We wanted to live the life of the theater, we thought we were already budding actresses, and that desire was like a command to observe, like spies, every detail of the way women behave in various circumstances. We took a dip in the river and we drifted around in a rowboat, but toward evening we thought we'd like to linger on and take a look at the women we'd heard about, who gathered outside that Grove every summer to give the men some pleasures they weren't getting inside, where no women were allowed, not even their wives.

We went into a hotel bar and I ordered only mineral water with lime and Josie ordered a Bloody Mary. She was twenty-two and she got a kick out of going into bars on her own, any bar from the low-down ones in the Mission District, where our families lived, to the elegant ones in the Nob Hill hotels. Some women in that bar thought we were moving in on their territory, a couple of girls showing off how young they were, and one woman demanded in a low voice that we move along. Josie told the woman to get lost. I didn't see one beauty among them, though at first glimpse of one and another I thought I did. Several of those women were old enough to be our mothers, and Josie said she wished her own mother looked so good. We'd heard that some women met the same man year after year and that arrangement seemed to me more exciting in a meaningful way. We watched them while pretending not to, and we could feel in our own bodies their kind of acting style, when sometimes you can't help but exaggerate yourself.

The first time I ever saw him in person was when he came into that hotel bar with his bodyguard. He looked familiar, of course, but almost every man there looked familiar. There was a likeness about them even though they were each different, tall or short, fat or thin, and some appeared kind of stiff, as though they were wearing braces for a fallen organ or a bad back. The bodyguards were like younger brothers, looking mean enough and sharp enough to protect an older brother who the world thought so valuable, but what I saw in their eyes was a blankness waiting to be filled with scenes of death.

These two, the man and his bodyguard, sat at a table and looked around as if they'd come out the gate just to see how the neighbors were enjoying the summer night. His glances kept coming back to Josie and me, but then I had to admit he was looking more at me than at her. Then his bodyguard came over and asked if we'd like to sit at their table. Josie said we'd think it over, and he went back to his big brother.

We didn't know whether to pretend we were like the other

women and back-off at the last minute or let them know right away that we had just dropped in there for drinks. I didn't like the idea of pretending we were like the other women. Pretense came too close to how I was really feeling, that I might want to be like them, not forever if that's how it was with them, but just for one night.

Unreal, sitting at a table with a man who was beyond other men, the way movie actors seemed to me then and presidents and men in high positions in foreign countries. So we sat with him and his bodyguard and I was right across the table from him. He didn't ask me to change chairs with his bodyguard until he looked so long at me I became so self-conscious I couldn't speak and my smile was like a facial cramp. I had this fear, this conviction, that he could read my mind and was learning about how my father and Josie's father, who both worked on the waterfront and, at union meetings, made a lot of loud criticisms of everybody in the government. Then he told his bodyguard, who was on his right side, to move to where I was sitting so I could come and sit beside him.

For a long time while I sat beside him he didn't say anything to me, and I thought that once I'd done what he wanted me to do, come closer, then he didn't think so much of me anymore. I thought I'd get up and take a walk down by the river, where there were people in rowboats out on the dark water and colored lights and far music and, over on the opposite shore, people talking and laughing on the little private wharves among the dark rushes. I figured that if I excused myself and got up and left them I'd like myself for doing that, because I didn't like myself obeying this silent man.

His fingers on his glass of vodka were long and slender, the nails very clean and glossy, and while I was wondering why I liked his hands and why I shouldn't like them, I was wondering how they'd feel, his hands on me. Then he touched my fingers as if he were counting them slowly, as if I were a child being taught how to count.

"I've got two sons," he said, "but no daughters, and I haven't been this close to a very young girl for one hell of a long time. I'm around so many old farts I forget that everybody was young once." He had taken my wrist. "I didn't catch your name."

I gave myself one I chose at that moment for its upper-class sound. "Kimberley," I said.

"You look more like a Magda," he said.

I said, "A what?"

He said, "You look Slavic. Russian? Rumanian? Green eyes, cheekbones, all that. The women there are seductive without half-trying. Comes naturally. Would you mind if I called you Magda?" His head was bent so he could see how I was taking his suggestion and I didn't want his face so close. "Women are believers. They know the rewards to be had for believing. So believe me when I tell you you're lovely and your name is Magda."

I shook my head and tried to laugh. With that kind of flattery he was not very different from the young men in the coffee houses who are always trying to make you laugh for them.

But then he said, "Get serious."

It was like a command and I disliked him for it, but when I glanced into his face, so close, I saw that his expression was a confusion of desire and resistance. I'd seen it before on other men, that confusion, but with him it was a scowl that made him look older or made him look his age. He could be fifty. Without the scowl he could be younger.

"I *am* serious," I said and I was telling a truth about myself that I was not often given the opening to say, the truth that when I laughed and when I fooled around, my heart wasn't always in it. Then I had to clear up any misunderstanding about what I'd just said. "What I mean," I said, "is that I didn't come here to go to bed with anyone."

"What did you come for then?" he said. "In all seriousness?"

"We just came by," I said. "We were out for the ride."

He released my hand. Even then, early on, I sensed he had possession of certain ways to keep you guessing about his next move and prolong your discomfort. After a time he said, "Maybe you came for something you can't admit to."

"If I admit to thinking about it," I said, "that's not the same thing as going on and doing it."

"It's the same thing as imagining it," he said.

Then I felt as if I were back in school, back in some class where you're supposed to ask yourself if you're an ethical person and he was the taunting teacher, proving to you that you're not.

He took my hand again, he kneaded my hand, and I think he intended to be gentle but he was wearing a ring and it hurt. "If not tonight, we'll say tomorrow night," he said. "Time enough for you to give it more thought. You'll have a room, you'll have a suite if that's what they call it here in the boondocks. It will be in your name, Magda. But Magda what? What shall we give you for a surname? When I was a boy my grandfather was in the U.S. diplomatic service, an ambassador, and he liked to talk about Magda Lupescu, mistress of King Carol of Rumania. Must've been enamored of her himself. He might have slept with her before the King came along."

"It doesn't sound like me," I said.

"What name shall I give you if not Magda?"

Some of the women had already gone off with their men in tow. There were paper lanterns strung along near the ceiling, there was music floating by, there were women waiting in their summer dresses that could be slipped off so easily, and there were those women already lying with their men in this hotel and other hotels in the little towns by the river. Then to myself I admitted that I liked being told what name I was to be called by him.

On our way back to the city Josie told me she had imagined assassins running in and shooting the man and his bodyguard and both of us, too, just because we were there, and I wondered aloud that if what she'd feared had actually happened would our relatives be more appalled by our being there than by our deaths? And we laughed hysterically over that. On the long drive back through the dark forests we were smoking like crazy and ridiculing the women there and the men. But after a while we were quiet, and I was wondering if I would return by myself the next night as I had promised him. I thought that I'd always wondered about myself, I thought that's all I ever did, but that night I knew I hadn't wondered half enough.

The clerk at the desk told me there was no reservation in that name, and I pictured him deep within that Sacred Grove, taking a moment to wonder if I'd been slapped in the face already or was about to be. I was always to hold it against him, my humiliation in that little lobby, my being turned away as if I'd only dreamed up his desire. Down the road at another hotel I found a room reserved in that name, but I had cried, sitting in the car, off under some trees in the dark, and I was always to remember that rebuff as a trick he may have wanted to play on me. The window was wide open and a breeze from off the river was slipping the edge of the white curtains back and forth over the sill, the way a hand might do it. It was the middle of summer and night was not around yet except in the high, dark rushes on the other side of the river. I went down into the small terraced garden and step–by–stone step down to the river and I took off my sandals and stood ankle-deep in the clear green mossy water, on slippery stones. I had no lover at that time and knew that even if I had a lover I might have considered coming back anyway.

The hotels were alike, rustic country inns of timber from the redwoods. Up on a deck off the dining room women were sitting at tables, having their drinks. The encampment was so far within the hundreds of acres of forest you heard nothing of what was going on, none of their entertainment, no music, no speeches, and none of the revelry around the many tables where the men were dining at that hour. Even though there was a room reserved in the name he'd given me, up on the second floor, the top floor, and I could turn and look up and see the window of that room with the white curtains, I disbelieved. If he did not show up, *that* would be believable. Not believable was this girl in a cotton dress of blue and yellow flowers, musk perfume in her armpits and on her thighs — Josie's offering. I was not believable to myself and yet I *was* myself more than at any other time I could remember.

I didn't want to go into the bar or the hotel restaurant because I wouldn't be able to enter there the way Josie could, glancing at no one, sure that everyone was glancing at her. And I thought that if he had asked Josie instead of me, she would have come back too, but not because she was impressed by him or intimidated, as I was, or daring. She would have come back to amuse herself. And soon enough, she was making jokes about him, telling those jokes on the stage in a stand-up comedians' bar in the city. She was sleeping with the enemy, she told them, and in her own backyard. She got lots of laughs with that topic, and I laughed, too. The year was 1974, and most of the audience had been in marches against the war in Vietnam and read the underground weeklies that more often than not accused him of covertly bringing down this or that regime or uprising. She even went so far as to confess that, like Judith, a biblical heroine, she just might cut off his head while he lay sleeping beside her. I didn't laugh over that one.

She had lent me a silver flask, filling it with scotch. It had a

tiny silver cup for a cap and I was sipping out of that while waiting in the room for him. I wanted to fool myself into drinking
more than I thought I was drinking, because fear of him had
begun to creep its way home to me.

"I got rid of Billy Boy," he said. "The moron defending my life.
I'm afraid of those fellows. They could just as easily kill you as
save you."

Yesterday he'd had on a sport shirt with a little polo insignia
on the chest. This evening he had on an elegant linen suit. I
said, "You look like you're on your way to the White House rose
garden."

"I was invited," he said, "but I told the President I was spending the night with Magda Lupescu. He said Who? And I said she's
King Carol's mistress, Rumania, you know, and he said Don't get
us into another war. What's she like?"

I was in the chair and he came over and sat on the edge of the
bed, facing me. He had long, narrow legs that took up the space
between us.

"What's in the flask?" He took it from me, his long fingers able
to ease anything he wanted from somebody else's hold, and gave
it a close appraisal, smoothing it. "Art nouveau," he said. "Who
gave it to you?"

"King Carol," I said. "You know." But my face must have told
him how ridiculous I felt, acting that part.

He said, "Put that aside, will you? Did you have your supper?"

"No," I said.

"Why the hell not?"

"I don't know," I said.

"You want your supper up here?" he said. "Or do you want to
go down?"

"I want to go down," I said.

But neither of us moved. He didn't move and I didn't move.

Until he said, "We'll go down. Put on your shoes or they'll suspect us of you know what."

We sat across from each other at a little table that had a nice white cloth and while I ate my chicken salad he drank his cognac and told me about the doings in the Sacred Grove, the entertainments, the plays they put on, the rituals. He could be as mocking as Josie, except that his mockery had no pardoning in it like hers had, as if she were patting on the head whoever she was saying things about. The things he said were cutting and when you laughed you felt you were pouring salt into the victim's wound. But I liked his voice, it was melodious despite what he was saying, and I thought if he sang he'd impress, and I liked what I thought were broad A's that sounded like a stage actor's. Watching his mouth, his eyes, I began to see that he was good looking in his youth, and even up to yesterday, and even at that moment. And I saw that he knew how he looked and I even liked him for knowing.

"Rack of lamb," he said. "A thousand lambs sacrificed for their racks. Do you speak French?" I shook my head, and he said, "Well then, I can't interest you in the rest of the menu unless I translate and I'd rather not bother. I'm fluent, but that's a tricky language, conceals more than it reveals, gives rise to wacky philosophers. Can you tell me, why is it that Americans speak only American?"

"I guess it's the one that makes sense," I said. Then I heard what I'd just said and I laughed at myself.

"Once I was driving drunk," he said. "Not one time but the time a cop pulled me over, and he asked me to recite the English alphabet and my head said to me You can't, boy, you're not English, and I said to the cop Will the American alphabet do?"

"Did it do?" I asked and knew right away that I wasn't supposed to carry on his joke for him.

"All the racks we could eat," he said. "And let's not forget the

Escargots Brillat-Savarin, named after that French philosopher
who ate nine hundred and two at one sitting and lived. And what
was the wine with those plump little snails? Was it a *Meursault
Blagny?* Our hosts here in these glades, our *nouveau riche*
California bumpkins, offer up the best cuisine in the world. But
their guests, their honorable guests, do they know what they're
eating? They do not. They're the world's top dogs, you see, so
they just gobble up everything set down before them."

"Why do you go there?" I said.

"Go there?" he said. "I don't *go* there. I *belong* there. They
can't do without me. I'm the life of the party."

He saw that I was picking at my salad and so he ordered
another drink, and because the waiter was slow in coming to our
table he called him back and ordered two of the same. When the
drinks came, he slid one glass towards me.

"What do you know about me?" he said.

I didn't know what he meant so I couldn't answer.

He said, "What if a fat Sheik out of Saudi Arabia called you
over and said your name was the Queen of Sheba. Would you be
waiting in that bed for him?"

"I wouldn't be impressed," I said.

"I impress you?"

Why did he want me to answer that when I had already
answered him with my presence?

"Ever meet anybody who was graduated cum laude, all that,
from Harvard? Never did? Ever know a corporate attorney who
stood up before the highest court of this land four times and won
every time? Never did?"

"Never did," I said.

"Good," he said. "He would've bored you to death."

Then he went into another silent phase that I thought was
cruel, closing himself off from me because I was the boring one.

"I want to go back to the room," I said.

On the way up the stairs I slipped my fingers in between his fingers because I had begun to suspect that he was afraid of *me,* something hard to believe. I gave him the key and he tried to unlock the door with his left hand, his free hand, and dropped the key and picked it up and tried again, laughing down in his throat. I took the key from him and with my right hand, my free hand, I opened the door. I opened the door and I closed the door, my back to him, and he came up against me and held me around and his hands smoothed me down, clasped me where he wanted to, and turned me towards him.

I was turned toward him from that night on. No matter what I was to know about him, no matter that I was to agree with Josie and our friends that he and his friends spread chaos and death in the world, he was always able to turn me towards him.

We did not draw apart until after one o'clock, when the air was cooling down and we began to hear the river, how the river at night seems deeper, swifter, riskier.

"They'll miss me," he said.

It's what a man says if his wife and family are waiting for him to come home, and I pictured all those men, CEOs, Ex-Presidents, Generals, Foreign Princes, all waiting up for him in their pajamas.

"Especially at this hour," he said, "when Georgie's playing the piano for them. Nostalgic stuff, piano bar stuff, some what they think is classical thrown in, and they hear it wherever they wander, cabin to cabin, drinks in hand, thinking life's been very, very good to them, and thinking their accomplishments will be memorable forever, and thinking that at least once in their lives they must have had some great sex but they're not sure because they don't know how it compares with everybody else's." He laughed down in his throat again, his kind of laugh that told you he was pleased with thoughts you'd never be let in on. "I tell them they're bunglers, I tell them they haven't accomplished a goddamn iota of what they think they have. I tell them they've lost the war and lost the world along with it. . . ."

I was listening and I was thinking that his way of talking to those men, who were congratulating themselves on a balmy summer night for what they hadn't accomplished and thought they had, must be like the way he made love to me, sure in himself that he knew more than anyone else about the art of accomplishing whatever you wanted. And he *did* know.

He drew himself up against the headboard, found his cigarettes and offered them to me. I drew myself up beside him but I felt so dazed, so dazzled, all I could do was put up my hand to refuse them and slide back down again. He stroked my hair, he stroked my face as he sat above me, smoking, and while I lay there I did not know where I was, I did not know where in the world I was.

Within those two weeks of what he called the Immortals Rest and Recreation, I came back four times to spend a night with him. Before him, I had stayed out nights with lovers and at other times, too, when Josie was on stage in a bar and after the bar closed we kept on joking with the others and I went home with her and slept in her apartment. So my father had no clue about where I was those nights I spent with him. If my father had ever learned he would have been angry of course and not only because it was an arrangement he would have said cheapened me, but also because whenever he heard that man's name, before I ever met him, he cursed him as a matter of course and wished him dead.

After that night we met in a house that was made available to us for the times we were there. Once, when I drove up earlier than usual, I saw a man who might have been the owner, a burly, gray-haired man in army fatigues, getting into his Mercedes. One summer, when the encampment was over and everyone had flown off, we stayed on in that house for a couple of days and nobody knew where he was. The newspapers rumored that he was in Bahrain, meeting with an Israeli arms dealer. A big house on the river, where you could walk down a grassy slope to the water and get into a long rowboat. One night I laid some cushions down in that rowboat to make love there, but he said he felt targeted out in the night with his back to the universe. He laughed in his way when he said that, but he meant it, and we walked back up to the house.

A year after he died I came back just to look around and see where I'd been and who I'd been. The flood had reached as high as the windowsill of that room on the second floor, the top floor, where I'd spent that first night with him, and the hotel had put up a little marker there to show how high the waters had come. The house where we'd spent those other nights was up for sale, and a woman realtor took me around to see it. I asked her why it was on the market, and she told me the owner was residing down in Panama. She laughed about that, and I didn't know why, then. Empty, all that ugly oversize furniture gone, and green-black mildew fringing the plush carpeting in the rooms downstairs and even on the stairs and up in the bedrooms. She took me down into a studio on the lowest floor where I'd never been. It was papered in gaudy colors and I saw how high the waters had reached, all the way up the walls to the ceiling, that year the rains went on for so long the river swept over its banks and flooded the town.

He had called me when he heard about that devastation. He said he was in Bethesda hospital, he said his body had turned traitor on him, that his body was like a counterspy, undiscovered until the damage was done. He asked me if the Sacred Grove was flooded and I said I didn't know. He said it was about time for God to send down another flood. He said he had warned them and they had failed to heed his warnings. Some apparatus to help him breathe helped his laugh along. That flood year was 1982. He died when the water began to recede. I saw both news items in the same day's paper.

The name of that woman who had enraptured his ambassador grandfather was always the name he called me by. No other name, not even my own. It came from his family history and I was convinced at that time that he was more entitled to a history than I was. I looked her up in some European history books and found a picture of her strolling in Paris with that ousted King, and she's wrapped in a coat with a big fur collar. They're both very Twenties stylish and they've got that look of historical notoriety that only the nobility can claim. Her face is so small in that photograph I couldn't tell how closely I resembled her, so he might have imagined a resemblance for his own purposes. He must have wanted to set himself apart, in an inviolably aristocratic way, from the other revelers in that Sacred Grove, and apart from me, too, from who I was with my own name and my own life.

I WANTED TO be able to call *his* name, but an intimate name only he and I knew. When Josie began to claim his real name for her comedy act, I was able to keep him separate from the man she was satirizing, because by that time I had given him another name she knew nothing about, and beyond that name I had so much more to give him than she could ever imagine.

non~fiction

The Naked Luncheon

SHE DESCENDS from the ceiling, down through a round hole that is draped with red velvet around its edges and with gold fibrillar loops of braid. The gilded piano that, during the preliminary performances of two orange-and-black fringed dancers shuffling and shaking, has appeared to float from the ceiling, now descends slowly on its tracks and cables; it is her support, her special piano with its insides removed. Visible first are the high-heeled beige pumps, then the ankles, the calves, the knees, the thighs of the turning legs, while the tension bounds upward, struck continual blows, like a strength-measuring machine at Funland, by the amplified fanfare from the four musicians on the stage. She is wearing nylon nude-colored tights, a French-cut bikini bottom of pink cloth that surprisingly reaches almost to the navel, a white wig of a starlet, page-boy cut, pearly-white lipstick, black awnings of eyelashes, and bare breasts rather large for her small body and a trifle more pendulous than globular. She is in constant motion, after the blasting introduction when the piano rests at last on the floor, and the dancing figure is made to appear twelve times faster by the spotlight that goes on and almost off constantly, reminiscent of the unnerving light on the top of a police car. The music blares, the words are unseparated. It is sound beyond sound so that only the impact of the waves is felt; one is caught in the din like a mouse in the amplified guitar. She moves the pearly mouth like Monroe; it opens but no word is heard in the din. There is something silent and pantomimic about the frantic figure within the blasting music as if it danced in the unreal center of a hurricane. After a kind of climax involving both music and body, the figure calms, the piano begins to rise. Up goes the white wig through the ceiling, up go the breasts, up go the legs. Carol Doda disappears, and once again the piano stands against the ceiling on air while the crowds along the sidewalk are ushered in by flashlight and half the audience rises and moves out from the darkness, illuminated on its way by a light from somewhere that turns the white shirts of the men a luminescent violet as if a globe burned within each chest.

HE PUTS INTO my hands a jigsaw puzzle. After it is assembled it will be a giant color photograph of Carol Doda, the same as on the cover of the box, facing front in a purple, topless swimsuit, one arm up and one arm down, pale hair straight to her shoulders, and on the crown of her head a red-and-purple spray of feathers. The man who gives me this gift is the biggest press agent I've ever seen in the smallest office I've ever seen, once a broom closet, perhaps, or a toilet when The Condor was a bar called the Black Condor. Expanded now into a nightclub, The Condor has a red-brick facade, arched windows with red glass, and fringed shades, and this triangular office in which I am wedged forms part of the jut at the corner of Broadway and Columbus. The desk is miniature and so is the typewriter; once, for a time, a three-foot midget served as master of ceremonies and this may have been his sanctum, but times have changed. In one corner are shelves piled with newspapers and magazines, and when the big man stands on a cane chair to bring down a newspaper from the top shelf it is almost unbelievable.

"On June 17, 1964," he begins, as if it were a world-shaking date. He was at the house of his boss, Gino, watching television. It was the time when the topless swimsuits were being introduced by the newspapers, and on the front page of the *Chronicle* that day was a photo of a four-year-old girl wearing one. "You want to know how to pack the place?" he asked his boss. "No four-year-olds," said Gino. At that time Carol Doda was a waitress at The Condor who did some dancing on a piano that stayed on the floor. Unfortunately, President Johnson was about to campaign in the city the first time she danced topless. "We couldn't get coverage," the press agent recalls. But notoriety came by way of a disc jockey who, through the glass of his booth, saw the topless suit held up by Gino, and the second night the place, as predicted, was packed. Within forty-eight hours Big Al's and The Off Broadway went topless, and not long after that a host of other clubs in North Beach—among them the El Cid, the Galaxie, Pierre's, Tipsy's, and several jigger-size bars around the periphery, where the only entertainment before had been the sour humor of the habitués.

"Some people are saying that her breasts are silicone," I begin, hesitantly.

It was he who gave out the secret, he admits. He gave it out, three months after injections were begun, to a columnist whose observations are as essential to a great many in the San Francisco area as their Librium or their Dexedrine, and now, passing by the even longer lines before The Condor, one hears the word silicone in questions and in answers. "She was mad at me at first," he admits, this admission as eager as the other, "but now she's glad to talk about it. Let's face it, when you go from a 34 to a 44 you can't keep it a secret. When a woman grows like that it's like getting pregnant. They call her Miss Silicone of 1965." I fail to ask who *they* stands for. "It sounds cruel," he admits, "but she doesn't care because this is what the public wants and this is what it's getting. This is the sex symbol that Hollywood didn't build."

She is also, I am told, the Pinup Girl of the Year for the men aboard the aircraft carrier U.S.S. *Kittyhawk,* who have requested a photograph of her to accompany them, as their letter puts it, on their "cruise to Vietnam." He will oblige with five thousand photographs. "Isn't that quite a number?" I ask. "They can give out the extra ones when they get to Vietnam," he replies.

Just as a matter of curiosity, because he is not yet thirty and has to his credit, already, this burgeoning of the entire North Beach, I ask him about his past. As the spirit behind Personalities of California, an enterprise quiescent now because of his involvement at The Condor and other topless clubs, he put professional athletes — wrestlers, baseball and football players — into supermarkets for autographing appearances. The women, he claims, loved it, they flocked in. "This old woman brought her Bible for Pepper Gomez to sign." As I leave the broom closet I see Tony, one of the three owners of The Condor, sitting, with a beatific smile, under a Gay Nineties chandelier.

WHETHER YOU are man or woman, there is an initial shock on finding yourself surrounded by nude women, or women who appear in the dim and nude-color light to be nude. At The Off Broadway, as your eyes grow accustomed to the half-dark and to the bareness, you are then able to perceive pointed gold pasties over nipples, nylon flesh-colored tights, bras on some and rayon or nylon panties such as can be picked up on a Macy's bargain table, stretch girdles and two-piece swimsuits, and to perceive, within bras or behind the spangled pasties, small breasts and medium-sized breasts along with the larger ones, and even a hollow chest from improper posture, and, within a girdle, a protruding belly as after a childbirth. They are, at second and third glance, very human and as if in a dormitory, running around to find their clothes. These are the performing non-performers, some at ease, one sweetly pigeon-toed and awkward, with a touch of humiliation where the clothes used to be, standing to take an order with a kind of protective slumping-in of pelvis and breasts, and these are the ones who are being ridiculed in print by another columnist, this one minor, who demands bodily perfection of the girls who serve him his breaded veal cutlets while his own imperfections are concealed beneath his tailor-hung suit.

Voss Boreta, The Off Broadway owner, with the smooth, dark face of the nightclub owner in any movie, talks with happy accommodation about the trials as we sit across from each other at a table that affords a view of the large and low-ceilinged room filled with the usual well-dressed couples and small groups of men and lone men, served by waitresses everywhere bare and bumping and easing by, and engaged by five convulsive girls on as many platforms all around the room, in net trousers and no more except shoes, and by the Beatle-like group on the stage and a long, lean blonde vocalist in a trance and yellow pajamas who dances incessantly as she sings. For several days in the Spring of 1965 the trials were given the front pages, the TV newscasts, and the gossip columns, and those persons who, before, were not aware of the preponderant importance of the topless dancers over other figures of the world scene were now made aware. And when the judge and the jury, upon his advice, ruled that the topless conduct was not outraging of public decency and the girls removed their covering again, there were even larger crowds on the sidewalks waiting for the ones inside to come out.

Before the nighttime topless fashion shows, The Off Broadway booked top or near-top entertainers, and then had topless fashion shows at lunchtime, parading the girls only around the tables. When the arrests began, Boreta at once staged a fashion show at night. In all, he was arrested three times. "We paid Trini Lopez $7500 a week," he tells me. "It's like — fill up a bag and give it to Trini. The total payroll, for him and everybody else, was about $13,000 a week. Now we're even more packed and the payroll is $7000, total." The dancers, still in a frenzy up there on their platforms, after what seems to be close to half an hour, not varying their routine but at least changing platforms, are paid $25 to $30 a night. The waitresses get $12.50 and their tips. There are thirty-eight girls employed on two shifts, and if Boreta runs short his brother supplies him. "My brother's got The Cellar. Before topless, if he got twenty people a night he was lucky. Now he can't handle them all. Chris Boreta — running for Board of Supervisors."

The stage is now clear for the fashion show, and there appears a tall and slender model with champagne-color hair, a gliding walk, and eyes that appear to glow on and off. The yellow-pajamas vocalist, now in the hatcheck booth with a microphone in her hand, parodies the commentary of a *haute-couture* show as the model glides across the stage in a green dress with a neckline so plunging it bares the breasts and the navel. She is a dancer from Las Vegas and so is the model who follows her, very tall, very slender, in a silver-grey dress that appears to be conventional. It is, however, a trick dress, for once on the stage she gives it a graceful tug and down comes the top. On the white-painted brick walls are life-size photos of a bare Yvonne D'Angers. Now she herself appears from out the door that leads to the kitchen and to the dressing room downstairs, an incomparable and somewhat confounding fusion of eighteenth-century French courtesan and girlie-magazine model. The wig is high and as white as Christmas-tree snow, the lips pearly-white, the eyelids weighted with black canopies, the walk slow with a gliding jog in the hips, the breasts globular, glowing faintly, perhaps with lotion, under the transparent lavender chiffon. Off in a corner of the room there is a glass stall where once a girl showered in what was called champagne. It is now a dressing room where Yvonne strips down to nothing behind white translucent curtains as the light inside dims down. In a red baby doll she emerges, rubs her back against the pillar at the edge of the stage, and, with utmost grace, lowers the top. Finding something amusing in the uplifted faces of the men below her, she laughs to herself, her breasts shaking with perfect timing. Now she lies down on the chaise longue that is covered with white fur, her legs up along the pillar, her breasts down almost under the chins of the nearest patrons, while the microphone voice, which strangely now appears to be Yvonne's mind in interior monologue, cautions *Don't touch. Just look.* She shifts position, she chooses one close patron and beckons slowly with the forefinger, and now the voice begins to make moaning, panting, husky sighs. *Hi, there, tiger. How are you? Get up, are you resisting? I'm sure you've bragged about it for years. Now stand up and do something.* The patron, a large man in a rather iridescent grey summer suit, won't stand up. *Oh, you really do have problems,* says the voice, and it is this terrorizing joke that brings him to his feet to bend his head over the face that, once again, is upside down on the edge of the chaise longue. Yvonne purses her lips upward as the patron bends his head downward; then, almost upon contact, the microphone voice, belonging again to the girl in the hatcheck booth, saying, "And that, ladies and gentlemen, was Yvonne D'Angers," sends her bounding up, running across the stage to her glass shower case, her mass of snowy hair shaking.

Down past the kitchen, down the stairs to the basement, and past a red-jacketed busboy playing solitaire standing up at the napery shelves, I come to the dressing room and find Yvonne settled nude in a chair before her dressing table, brushing a fake nail on the forefinger of the blonde Las Vegas girl. The fingernail, held up for my inspection, appears afflicted with a humpy cornification. "Then you file it down," explains the Las Vegas girl, "and put on the polish. Oh, yes, they last . . ." and each girl displays her long, gold-tipped fingers.

There are racks of garments, transparent and opaque, of many colors, a small couch, and on the dressing tables, among the jars and bottles, some Listerine mouthwash and a bottle of witch hazel. Around the large mirror before Yvonne are perhaps twenty photographs of herself. She tells me that her father sells Citroëns to the Persians, that when she was a schoolgirl in Paris she walked by the Moulin Rouge and saw a photograph of a nude couple in a fishnet and heard that suggestive things were done in the dance. "Oh, how I wanted to see that act," she tells me. It is her smiling, obliging history. The brunette model, who has been dancing on the stage upstairs, in a sequined crotch piece and high heels, a shuffle-footed, on-a-dime dance with graceful wavings of her arms, now runs in. She throws a transparent, yellow, ruffled capelet around her shoulders and sits on the sofa to combine her observations on Las Vegas with those of the champagne blonde, who is her room-mate. They were given, they tell me, a chance to tour with a troupe in Europe, but turned it down because of the dog quarantine in England. Their three sheepdogs would have been detained six months, and none of them could have borne so long a separation. Someone outside reminds the girls the show begins again in three minutes.

The atmosphere, the next day at noon, is slightly different at The Off Broadway. There are fewer women, no musicians, and in among the waitresses with their pasties and their girdles and their bras, as before, is one with a green-striped cotton dress and low heels. Had she come in late and found no time to remove her clothes? It was at her table I was given a chair by the hostess and I ask her why she wears a dress. "It's just that when I'm out among strangers I prefer to wear clothes." It has an anachronistic sound here, like a medieval superstition. She is unmarried, a girl with a guileless face, who hastens to tell me that she is not the only one, that another girl, who also worked there before the place went topless and who is now on vacation, also wears a dress. A plump girl with lingerie bra and girdle is standing nearby. "Why aren't you topless?" I ask her. "I don't believe in it," she answers. "I believe in illusion." Of an amiable girl with pasties and panties I ask how the pasties are made to stay on. "With surgical glue," she replies. And how do you remove them? "With an ouch." One of the girls is now gliding across the stage in an orange transparent gown. "She's got a beautiful face," says an elderly man to his male companions around a small table. "I'm interested in those things. I used to be a mortician." The amiable waitress appears to be in a state of discomfort; there is a hint in her arms of a need to hug herself. "I'm cold," she confides. I ask if there is a device for extending the nipples while one sleeps, as

I have noticed the extraordinary length of those on the model now passing among the tables. "They're the oddest nipples I've ever seen," the waitress agrees. "There may be a device, but I don't know of any." She has been a waitress for six years and has worked as a topless one for six months. "Are you molested by the men?" I ask. "No such luck," she replies and goes off to attend to her tables.

I turn my attention to the seven men at my table. They are all with a carbide company, the one across the table informs me, and one of the seven is telling the others about the salesman in the silicone division in San Francisco who sends out pictures of Carol Doda, before and after. Laughter follows this and jokes: "If I ever see silicone again, I'll recognize it," and, "You know what you'll hear now — Do you love me for my silicone or for myself?" The man across from me wears heavy glasses that appear to have behind them meditative eyes. No, it's not a convention, he tells me. Just a few people with the company from around the country. He himself is from New York. "Are they silicone?" he asks me as Yvonne passes by, and I tell him I am uninformed.

"In a sense," he comments, "it's like creating a freak in a circus. Nature did a grand job, better with some than with others. But one time people thought bleaching hair was gross, so maybe I'm behind the times. I'm a leg man, myself." He laughs. The others have left the table. He stands up, pats my shoulder. "It's just a joint with a gimmick," he says. What other products does his company manufacture? I ask. "Plastics, batteries, antifreeze, sapphires. . . ."

THE PLASTIC SURGEON I call on informs me that the injections of liquid silicone by means of a needle into multiple areas of the breast is regarded as unethical by the California Society of Plastic Surgeons, for whom he speaks. Since the use of the medical-grade silicone is not approved by the Federal Drug Administration, manufacturers cannot release it and those persons injecting silicone are using either an industrial grade or are obtaining some other similar type of silicone compound. Because the silicone is promising, however, the F.D.A. has approved the release of the medical grade to several university medical centers for use only in small areas of the body, with injections into the breast specifically excluded. The reason for this exclusion, he explains, is that the ultimate fate of the material in the body is still uncertain. For one thing, it may disguise the presence of a breast tumor, and, for another, experiments have shown that sometimes a portion of the material injected locally disappears and may be carried to other areas of the body. "Where it goes we don't know."

Some silicone, I learn from a chemical engineer-salesman, resembles a thick motor oil. Sand is the starting material and silicone is an organic, modified polymer of sand. It is called dimethylpolysiloxane. He himself has not sold silicone to doctors, he assures me, but he knows that doctors purchase it anonymously. "It's as easy to buy as milk," I am told. "Any large-volume item is impossible to keep track of. So the medical profession, if they dictate their ethics, will have to do the policing, not the industry." His company has no medical-grade silicone, but the industrial grade, he is sure, is as pure. Its other uses? I ask. "Silicone rubber, used by the aerospace industry and by the missile industry for seals and gaskets. And by the urethane industry in foam for furniture, automobiles, insulation. . . ."

DAVE ROSENBERG, the press agent, is waiting at Enrico's, inside, past the customers sitting in the open around the small, marble-top tables, each with its single rose in a vase. Surprised to find him there because I had thought the interview was to be between Carol Doda and myself, I realize, as we sit down to wait for her, that his presence should have been expected; he is an integral and anxious part of her image. He wears a sky-blue sweater and orders a double Coke. "You heard of George and Teddy and The Condors?" he asks me. "We got a new record, a 45, *Ain't That Loving You, Baby?* We're going to put them up in a helicopter — George and Teddy — and drop 10,000 ping-pong balls on San Francisco. I get home at three in the morning and sit up thinking, thinking, always thinking up new ideas."

She comes in smiling, swinging a black bag, wearing a black-and-red poor-boy sweater, dark-green bell-bottom trousers, and high-heeled black pumps. Dave has told me that she is a frustrated person. I bring up the subject and he answers first. "She gets all kinds of publicity. She gets more publicity than almost anybody except maybe Mamie Van Doren or Jayne Mansfield. She wants to go places. Let's face it, I want to go places, too."

"I think about it day and night," says Carol. "I don't want to be topless forever. I like productional shows — Las Vegas, New York, Europe. I've been in *Der Spiegel* magazine in Germany, the London *Times,* and *Spectator* — they know me in Europe. Anybody else would be touring, but I'm still at The Condor. They helped me get this far, but now they're holding me back. Something's got to explode."

I bring up the possibility that in a year from now every major city in the country will have topless dancers and the fact of her being the original one might have no bearing in the presence of hundreds or thousands of other topless dancers. Since she has no manager, I suggest that she find one. She agrees. "I have to go on to greater heights . . ." and, turning to Dave, she suggests that he phone to New York.

"You could phone Gypsy Rose Lee," he proposes. "You could ask her about a manager." Carol was on Gypsy's TV program, he informs me, and answered questions about the silicone. "At the

end of the show Gypsy says to the women, *The bus for the silicone doctor loads out front right after the show.* It was banned in L.A."
He tells me that he gets around three calls a week from women who want to know where they can get the treatments.

"Why do women do it . . ." I begin.

"Do they do it for men or for themselves?" asks Dave of Carol, interpreting my question with fewer complications than I had intended for it.

"Not for men," says Carol. "I do it for myself. Men are animals. They don't care how a woman looks."

"We care, we care," protests Dave, shifting his weight in the small chair. "Some beautiful women, they look gorgeous with makeup. You see them in the morning and you want to give them a broom and send them on their way."

"Is there," I ask her, "any resentment? How does it affect you erotically?"

"What's that mean?" she asks.

"It means love," explains Dave.

"No," she replies, musing on resentment. "Because it's part of me. It's me. It becomes a part of yourself. When I see my old pictures I tear them up."

The three of us leave Enrico's, passing two men at one of the tables on the edge of the sidewalk, who lean out to watch her after she has gone by. Carol and I, walking behind Dave for a few yards, are both obscured from oncoming pedestrians. It isn't until they get past him that they see she is there.

THERE IS A place called Mother's. On its windows are painted, in luminous red and black, nude women standing life-size, reminiscent of stained-glass figures. One enters into a chamber of uterine-red walls, rippled and folded in bas-relief as if frozen in the midst of contraction. In the men's room, I am told, there is an *assemblage* of tin soldiers and comic strips, and in the ladies' room there is one of broken dolls. Maria is introduced as the "labacious" dancer, or perhaps the microphone plays tricks. She is the girl who has been sitting at the bar in a black and silver kimono. "No dogs," warns a patron against the wall, a young man with the face of an aristocratic alcoholic. "No dogs," he repeats. Maria, growing at once agitated by the music, wears a bra that is not a bra. It acts as a spangled shelf for the bare breasts. She rolls her buttocks and strokes her breasts at the suggestion of the drummer who is singing out his many directions. And here, as in other clubs, the dancer's body seems to be undergoing a kind of frantic confinement in a yell leader's psyche of close-together legs and ebullient school spirit. There are no bumps, no grinds, there is no carnality here or impending carnality, and perhaps that is what is missing most because it is what we are led to expect. There are only the routines, up and down the block, of pistol pantomime with index fingers from the hips, of shotgun loading, of pony riding to music playing that very moment on a dozen radio stations in the area, and there are patrons' Sing Alongs, with clapping above the head, similar to Simon Says. What *is* present is something of Pop Art, the multi-static squares of race-cars, canned soup, pie wedges, motorcycles, and a movie star nude on a hamburger, what *is* present is an obstinate child-like innocence of the same kind that puts a fighting-cock cartoon on the helmets of our bomber pilots and drops toys a day after bombs. Over at the Red Balloon, one swoops down a slide, to the blast of a horn and the pop of rifles from the shooting gallery, into a carnival where patrons can throw balls at a target to knock a topless girl out of bed and, for a moment, into view, and where strip poker is played for a dollar a hand and the only one who strips is the girl. And down at the corner at Benny the Bum's, a small bar, Joyce, the Negro waitress, in black boots and net over-blouse, snaps her fingers and shuffles on a little platform, some-times lifting her blouse in a parody of the other *haute-couture* parody with, "Now I'm gonna show my lil tiddies."

UP IN THE dressing room at The Condor, in the few minutes before her last appearance for that night, Carol Doda removes the simple black dress she has been wearing while chatting with the patrons at the bar. Underneath, ready for the act, are the flesh-color tights, and tonight there is a grey bit of bikini bottom with what appears to be a silver braid bobbing at the back. She turns before the mirror. "I remind myself of a horse," she says, laughing, flipping up the braid. "A beer-wagon horse or the ones that pulled the fire trucks." She has, I notice, a beautiful back.

Was the silicone her own idea?

"It was suggested to me," she answers me. She was afraid at first, she thought about it a month, but the doctor reassured her. "But I paid for it myself. *I* paid for it." She describes for me how it's done. "Once a week for a year. It's pumped in with a big needle, like a horse needle. At first it feels too firm. It's like breast now, it feels soft."

She tells me about a letter she has received that day from the mother of a teen-age boy. It has upset her. She tore the letter up, but the pieces are still around if I want to read it. Reverends write to her, informing her that she needs help. There is a fragility to her face, the makeup appears to weigh on it, and there is a quick, natural animation in her gestures. What hurts her most, she tells me, are the kids calling her nasty names along the street and the women calling her a witch. She has no friends, her girl friends turned against her. "You know why? They're afraid. They don't want me to be famous. But I must have something that has to *be*. I know why Marilyn killed herself. Everybody steps on you. Judy Garland, who knows all about emotional upsets, was by to see me. And Gypsy Rose Lee, she came by with her little Mexican dog."

The dressing room looks like a McAllister Street second-hand store. There is a couch and a dresser that in 1930 were probably bargain pieces, old grey lockers that might have been salvaged from a ship. Shoes of the other two girls, now dancing below, lie about on the floor; clothes are thrown over chairs. From below rises the fanfare for her descent. We climb into what appears to be a tunnel and run along in it, bent over. It is a passageway four feet high and about that wide. "It's like being in the war," she says. "You know, a foxhole." We come to a hole in the floor. It is the hole through which she descends, a square one made to appear round from below with the use of a hoop from which hang the red velvet folds and the gold loops. Obviously she is standing on something solid, for she doesn't fall through, feet first. She descends, checking on the stability of her eyelashes and the artful dishevelment of her bangs even as her ankles and legs are beginning to appear to the audience below and the music moans and bellows and throws itself against the ceiling. On my knees I peer over the edge. She is almost down, and as I gaze on the crown of her head I am startled to see the fabric of the wig in which are rooted the white tendrils of hair.

There, gazing down through the hole at the dancing figure in the flashing light, I am reminded again, as I have been reminded of it in the presence of the other bewigged and breasty entertainers, of the story *Gogol's Wife*, by the Italian writer, Tommaso Landolfi. The wife is a balloon doll that Gogol pumps up to the proportions that he wishes, more on one day, less on another, with variations of each part. The color of her hair is changeable, on other areas in addition to her head, and even the color of her skin. But after some years of this ideal mating, while he is entertaining a guest, and the wife, plump that night and blonde, is sitting on a pile of cushions, she speaks: "I want to go poo-poo," she says slyly. It is the beginning of the end. She begins to show signs of aging, grows bitter and religious, and bears a child. And so, torn between love and disgust, he is driven at last to destroy her. He pumps her up until she explodes and is no more.

March 1966

The Last Firing Squad

THERE WILL BE no names, neither of the men in the picture nor of the towns where they now reside. Since it is imperative to name the state where, uniquely, the firing squad is a mode of execution in civil trials, the state is Utah, and counties and towns where crimes and executions took place will also be named, for those names are known already. But the two riflemen and the captain — three men out of eleven — who consented to pose and to recall that morning in May of 1956 when they came up from Iron County to the state prison for a double execution, will bear no names and no features. That is the way they wanted it. Out in the cold field covered with sage and thistle, with a far background of cedar on the low hills, with the high, red escarpments of a geological fault, and, beyond the fault, the Rocky Mountains, only the shapes of the men are made known; the rest is wilderness.

Out of Las Vegas in the clear and early morning, going north through the desert to Utah, the bus passed a metal sign, *Caution, Ammunition Xing,* and the Pago Pago Trailer Court. We were surrounded by a flat desert of inert brown, rimmed by low ridges of the same color. On the window glass at my left, superimposing itself on the far brown mountains, floated the blue-grey reflection of the mountains to the right of the highway. There was nobody in the miles of stillness, and when the bus passed two surveyors with their red-legged tripod, for a fraction of a second they appeared to be native to the desert. Against the pale sky, once in a long while, the dingy habitations of man, towered over by gold winter trees, came into view. An Indian woman, round-faced, stood by the door of a trailer that was long ago hitched to the earth. A flock of small, confused birds, desert brown, flew straight with the highway toward the bus, scattering at the last moment. The telephone poles were rough, fresh-colored, with traces of branches. After hours of flat desert the bus climbed; the plants, low and bleached before, grew thicker and taller, there was more green to their greyness and there were more branches to the low trees that began to appear a few miles back, bare trees except for spiky green leaves at the tip of each lifted branch — a tree named Joshua by the emigrant Mormons after the biblical figure who led the way to the Promised Land, and in the ditches along the highway grew a high, thick sage. In all that brush the wind was more evident, and then, ahead, there was a sight of rust-red buttes, beyond them more brown mountains, veined with snow, and, perhaps half a state away, white mountains.

Over the intersections of the town, tinsel glittered in the sun.

A pickup truck passed with deer antlers showing above its high sides. The Iron County sheriff's office, up on the second floor of a small hollow-sounding building, its staircase painted battleship grey, was crowded with desks and filing cabinets; covering one wall and part of another were descriptions and pictures of wanted men.

The sheriff, a tall, very erect elderly man, and his deputy, a tall, lean, slightly slouching young man, both of them amiable and both with the light-brown hair and pale eyes common to that region, had already by long distance put the seekers in touch with the sought after by supplying the name of the man who had been captain of the double firing squad. The murder, for which two men were executed at the same time, took place, the deputy explained, in Beaver County; a young man, a gasoline-station attendant, was shot by the two during a robbery. But because "feelings were so high" in Beaver County, the trial was held in Iron County and the sheriff of that county, a man now deceased, mustered the firing squads from men who volunteered. The Utah legislature has, since then, shifted the responsibility for assembling squads from the sheriff of counties where trials are held to the warden at the state prison.

Twenty years ago, the sheriff recalled, he had himself served on a firing squad. The man he had executed had come from California and, after buying himself a pistol in Las Vegas, had shot a salesman from Salt Lake who had given him a ride north into Utah. "I was on the highway patrol at the time, and the sheriff asked me to come along. We went up to the old prison at Salt Lake and practiced on the rifle range. There were about two hundred spectators." I asked him how he felt about executing a man. "If I had to shoot a man, in the Army, it would bother me. I'd feel they were as good as myself. I was in the Army in World War I, and I didn't get out of the country. But for a scoundrel who bought his pistol for that purpose, I feel he had forfeited his right to live among human beings. It was like shooting a coyote. The coyotes killed four or five sheep a night, when my father ran sheep." I asked him if he knew how the others on the squad felt. "One of them got to drinking, afterward, and when he was drunk he'd say, 'I wish I hadn't gone in there.' But he was the one who had the rifle with the blank. I knew because I watched them put their rifles on the rack and I put mine down last, and then I felt each rifle and I knew he was the one because his was the cold one. It was that man who worried most about the execution." Why, I asked, did he not tell the other man that his rifle held the blank? "He might have felt I was lying to appease him."

In the street I was again aware of the wilderness surrounding the tinseled town; the high red rocks, veined with snow, rose directly behind the row of stores, and on the other side of the highway the flat plain reached for miles to a range of mountains. The impression got from the two amiable men was of a state with its citizens settled down to the day's work, to the years' farming and mining, settled down to the ways of the righteous, the criminals from elsewhere, entering and leaving on the highways that traverse the state. "The Mormon crime rate is lower than the national average. They come up from North Carolina, Texas, Tennessee, California," the deputy had informed me, speaking of the persons responsible for many of the major crimes in Utah. "Those two met in California and were on their way to Missouri to get rid of somebody one of them had a grudge against."

It is like a nation, the state of Utah. To ask anyone if he is a Mormon is a ridiculous question. The entire state is divided geographically by the Church, whose highest authorities convene at Salt Lake City, into stakes, with presidents and councils, and the stakes are divided into wards, and among the wards the bishops are many, not the robed kind, but farmers, mayors, miners, lawyers, anyone whom the Church presidency regards as worthy; though they may not be versed in theology, they are, with their advisory presence, persuasive of devoutness. The one I called on was an automobile dealer, watching, from his small office, a truck dumping a load of gravel onto his car lot in preparation for the winter snow.

"That's the Old Spanish Trail," he told me, nodding toward U.S. Highway 91, a few yards away. "The padres passed along there one hundred years before the Mormons." He was a red-haired man, his suit trim as a banker's, his face without expression, as if he were convinced that, were he to move a facial muscle, the movement would distract from the unwavering gaze. He was, he told me, chairman of the Presiding Bishopric that supervises the Church's welfare farm for needy Mormons, who work there or who are assisted by its produce. The Church has worldwide welfare projects — farming, the manufacturing of clothing, bedding, furniture, "everything that people need. It's the duty of the Church to look after its people, both spiritually and temporally. They're not well spiritually unless they're well temporally."

The bishop's son, who was twenty-four and who had served two-and-a-half years as a missionary in the Mormon missions of New Mexico and Texas, brought me the *Book of Mormon* in a red-brown, imitation-leather cover stamped with a gilt angel blowing a trumpet. It is the Church's history of ancient peoples, believed to be the Word of God translated by the young Joseph Smith of the village of Manchester, Ontario County, New York, from gold plates delivered over to him on the Hill Cumorah, their place of concealment adjacent to the village, by the Angel Moroni, who on earth had been the son of the chronicler Mormon, the exact date of delivery recorded by the recipient as September 22, 1827. Although "multitudes were on the alert continually" to wrest those tablets from his hands, as Smith notes in his preface, they remained safe until his task was done and the angel returned for them. From the Angel Moroni's visits, from the gold tablets, rose the Church of Jesus Christ of Latter-day Saints.

It rose also from a time of religious hysteria along the frontier and the Atlantic seaboard, when new churches, and sects and subsects, were born overnight, and congregations, as one historian has observed, went mad, "jerking, barking, jumping, hopping, dancing, prancing, screeching, howling, writhing in fits." Driven from place to place, from Missouri into Illinois, their farms burned, the men tarred and whipped, and Joseph Smith himself killed by a mob that stormed the prison in Carthage, Illinois, where he was awaiting trial for suppressing an apostate newspaper in the Saints' city of Nauvoo, the Saints fled across the continent to Great Salt Lake valley and settled there, all by themselves except for the Indians.

The bishop calculated that, of the state's population now, sixty-five to seventy-five percent is Mormon; perhaps fifty percent in Salt Lake City and much higher in the rural areas. "We believe in being subject to the secular laws," he explained when I asked for the Church's attitude toward the death penalty. "We're all over the world and wherever we go we abide by the laws of whatever state or country we're in." Is the secular law so secular — the one that decrees death — when so large a percentage of Utah is Mormon? I failed to ask the question; there may be a blind spot in that unwavering gaze, but it is not a blindness that afflicts only that one spokesman of that one Church in that one state.

There were few lights at night in the towns of southwestern Utah; beyond U.S. Highway 91, with its streetlamps, store fronts, and motel signs, the towns were dark, with a density of darkness unknown to the city. The house of the man who had been the captain of the two squads was, in the vernacular of the city, a tract house, though it may have been singular in that region, or one among a similar few. Just off duty, the captain had appeared at the motel door to invite me to his house, smiling, joking, "I hear you're looking for me," pleased with being sought after — a tall, robust man in the tan uniform of an officer of the law. By his side was a beaming man in a business suit who had come from another state, the first member of the firing squads to respond to the captain's call to assemble again. In the kitchen of the house all was modern; even the framed and embroidered Give Us This Day Our Daily Bread might have been a store-bought replica. On the table was a crocheted cloth and a candle, on the telephone stand a black-covered New Testament and a red-covered Seminary Song Book.

The cheerfulness of the captain's wife, a pretty brunette, appeared habitual, as if it were an attitude early learned as the most practical. The youngest son, four, in pajamas, played on the floor and climbed into a chair to sit at the table with the rest and listen incuriously to things beyond him. Present was a local attorney, a large man with a self-conscious shrewdness, his wife, and the photographer from New York in his raccoon-lined raincoat. Before each one was a tall glass of whatever was requested, either whiskey with water or water with whiskey, while the bottle remained on the sink counter, wrapped in its paper bag.

Across the table from me sat the man from another state, an officer in the juvenile-protective service and, at the time of the execution, on the highway patrol. When his beaming smile lapsed, a friendly, anxious scowl took its place. "I save grossly neglected children," he said. "The abused, the beaten, the exploited. When I took the job, everybody on the highway patrol said what do you want that job for? I get more satisfaction out of rescuing one snotty-nosed kid than I'd get out of bringing in the top ten men." He repeated this last sentence in a louder voice, as if still trying to justify that change to his friends. He knows by heart, he told me, many passages in the *Book of Mormon* and he has "felt the truth" of his religion.

"'Can you sleep?' people asked me. 'How can you sleep?'" He recalled the aftermath of the execution. "I felt uneasy and needed substantiation. To justify our participation we read Church articles, we saw things we wanted to see in them. I read that the First Presidency of the Church said: We sustain the people of Utah and if the people of Utah lay down the choice of execution, we uphold the laws."

Although a man may choose hanging, in Utah, most of the condemned men choose the firing squad, and that choice involves five executioners. The deputy sheriff had told me, of the squads from Iron County, "They all volunteered, but after a few months, a few years, you think it over and the anger or temper is gone, you forget the facts and remember Thou Shalt Not Kill. It worries them, killing somebody."

"One man went through a certain amount of hell," the man with the scowl went on. "He was sick, after. His brother said they should have professionals on the police force do the job. Four of us on the squads were law-enforcement men and so was the captain. The rest were civilians who were deputized. I said to the brother, Do you mean I kill a man every day?"

They began, then — the restless, joking captain who had not yet sat down and the man with the scowl — to recall the execution itself, and there was, in that neat tract-house kitchen with its atmosphere of neighborly assembling, with cartons of Chinese food warming in the oven, an impossibility of evoking more than a modicum of the oppressive excitement and dread of that occasion that may have been the most profound of their lives.

In the darkness of early morning they were called from their hotel room in Salt Lake City and driven to the new state prison at Draper, twenty miles away, in cars whose windows were covered over with newspapers. Their names withheld from the press and even from officials of their own county where the trial was held, that morning, men whose identities the citizens of the state concealed from themselves as a bad conscience is sometimes concealed almost out of existence. Still in the dark that they described years later as pitch dark, they were driven through the fields and in through the back entrance of the prison. There, between the wire-mesh fences that surround the compound, in that fifty-foot space between the fences, they assembled in a shack, a three-sided structure, its open side — open except for a forty-inch high wall — facing the other three-sided shack, some twenty feet away. Across the open end of the other shack, dimly lighted as their own, hung a burlap curtain and through it they could see two waiting chairs. Within the prison the convicts were making a great clamor, banging objects against the bars. The guards appeared with the two condemned men, each holding the hand of a Catholic priest. As the men were strapped in their chairs with arm straps, leg straps, waist straps, the two guards in the shack with the firing squads handed around the rifles, Winchester 30-30s. The squads had practiced firing in unison in Iron County the day before because, as the captain now recalled, "it would have been an atrocity if we hadn't shot together." Whatever is said to condemned men in their last minutes was said by the priests, and when the priests had stepped aside, the Iron County deputy sheriff read the execution order. Each man was asked if he had any last words and each said no. Long black hoods were drawn over their heads down to their chests, the doctor applied his stethoscope, and white targets, circles four inches in diameter, were pinned over their hearts. The floodlights came on, and with the coming on of the lights, the din within the prison ceased. The burlap curtain was removed, and the deputy sheriff, walking away from the hooded men, took off his Stetson, his signal to the captain, who called out his *Ready, Aim, Fire.* "It was just when the old sun come up over the old mountain," said the man with the scowl, across the table. "It was just sunrise."

"They burn everything after," said the captain. "They take everything out in the field — the two shacks are built on skids — and they burn it all."

ONLY TWO of the ten men of the two squads were persuaded by the man who had been their captain ten years before to accompany him in the morning to the motel where the photographer was staying. Although most of them still resided in southern Utah and the day was Saturday, only four, altogether, came, and they came late. With the alacrity of discomfort, they filed into the room: the jovial captain; the man from another state; another law-enforcement officer, in uniform, stocky, whose toughness seemed a parody and who might have been the youngest at the execution, perhaps barely over twenty-one then; and a man who appeared to be the most mature of the group and the most nervous, a civilian and a teacher. "We don't know how you'll write about us. We don't know if you're a conservative or an extremist," the man with the friendly scowl began. And the teacher's presence did not, he assured us, mean a willingness to be named or photographed. "If I had to do it over again, I'd do it," he explained. "But I don't want the kids at the school to see my picture. I don't want them to know." They filed out after only a few minutes, to confer together at another place, to persuade and dissuade, to ponder on repercussions. A fifth man came after they had left — the mayor-elect of a town some miles away. Told that the others had gone into conference, he left to join them and never returned. The coffee in the paper cups turned cold, and the photographer, with the possibility before him of nobody to photograph, considered setting up five rifles in the old cemetery at the edge of town. In the middle of the afternoon, three reappeared: the man from another state; the stocky officer; and the captain — the latter two with their uniforms covered by jackets, with Stetsons in place of their uniform caps.

Miles from town, out in the sage, they lined up with rifles before the camera on its tripod. About their gestures and their exchange of jokes was the not-unpleasant nervousness of notoriety.

"For a price we can fix the sun from going down," the stocky one said, and laughed. Although assured that his face would be in shadow, he refused to raise his chin. He borrowed a cigarette from the captain, the only one of the three who smoked, and clamping it between his lips, in the very center of his mouth, he moved it up, then down, changing its direction each of the innumerable times the photographer clicked the shutter, grimacing over it in order to be less recognizable.

"Where were you when the lights went out?" the man with the scowl asked the photographer from New York, and he, in constant attendance on his camera, had no adventure to relate about the night when the northeastern part of the country was plunged into darkness. "You know that woman who prophesied about Kennedy's assassination?" the questioner went on. "She prophesied that power failure. Only she said the Russians would cause it."

The day had been warm but the earth remained cold. Snow lay along the incline between the highway and the barbed-wire fence through which we had climbed. Once in a long while a car went by, usually a pickup truck. Way out on the field was a shack the color of white sky, and beyond it a large, golden patch of wild, crested wheat. The mud was thick, hardened by the winter sun, and a red-yellow color, sprinkled with rabbit dung and small, pale twigs.

On that day, a few hours earlier, Gemini VII had gone up. "What's your bishop say about space travel?" the man with the scowl asked the captain. "He's against it," said the captain, and the questioner made a scoffing face: "That's a Dark Age doctrine, to stay confined on earth. My bishop believes in man's use of his own intelligence."

The air grew cold as the sun neared the mountains. The man with the scowl recalled that when he was at sea, during the war, his brother sent him some sage; it was so fragrant he took it all around the ship. When the posing was done, the stocky one removed his pistol from the holster at his hip, removed the bullets from the pistol, took off his badge, and, in the last minutes of the clear light, demonstrated to all gathered around him how quickly he could draw. Again and again he dropped the badge, held at a level with his shoulder, and almost every time before the falling badge reached his waist, he had drawn his pistol from the holster and pulled the trigger.

NOT IN UTAH alone are executioners nameless and faceless, and some states grant them, along with their anonymity, further concessions to conscience. In Utah, one rifle among the five contains a blank cartridge, and in another state, where the electric chair is the means, three men pull levers, but only one of the levers releases the current; which man's hand actually did the job is never known to them. And along with the consideration shown the executioner has gone, hand in hand, the inventiveness to more swiftly dispatch the soul of the executed.

With instruments unavailable in the past, executions are now more scientifically accomplished, and so, it is assumed, more humanely, and with greater decorum. Upon the occasion of the first execution by electric chair, in Auburn Prison, New York, in 1890, the dentist inventor of the device declared, "We live in a higher civilization from this day." And although not all scientists learned in the effects of electricity on the human body agree that it is not torture, and although the body may be burned at the point where the electrodes are applied and a malodorous smoke may arise from under the helmet that holds the head electrode, although the body is thrown into convulsions, and although it is sometimes necessary that the switch be thrown again and again because the heart still beats dimly, and although, if the current is applied for half a minute, the heart may rupture, the lenses of the eyes fracture, although there are unfortunate peculiarities attendant upon the process, the electric chair is extolled for its increased benefits to its victims. To the octagonal steel-and-glass gas chamber in San Quentin, in California, a green carpet is laid down so that the condemned man need not walk his last steps on cold concrete, and he is kindly advised to breathe deeply to make it easier on himself. And although the victim may take eight, nine minutes to die, that method of execution results, it is asserted, in an almost instantaneous loss of consciousness. Unable to appreciate the benefits accruing to that process, one man, frail of build, broke loose from the straps before the cyanide pellets were dropped into the bucket of sulfuric acid under his chair, and ranged in a frenzy within the sealed chamber and, after guards were sent in to restrap him, again worked free of the wrist straps and the chest straps and was working free of the waist strap when the gas overcame him.

If the word easier belongs at all in the context of dying, then the more modern devices of death may grant an easier dying over methods of the past, some taking hours and even days, over quartering by four horses, over the gallows before the invention of the long drop, and before the selection of the most efficacious position of the knot by a conference of Irish surgeons; over burning at the stake; over breaking on the wheel; over drowning in pits; over the Iron Virgin of the Inquisition with a gilded halo around her head and an embrace of knives; over the rack; over the ax, before the guillotine, when the executioner did not customarily take but one stroke; over pressing by iron weights; over flaying; over boiling; over stoning; over the caldron turned upside down on the victim, with mice within so that the fire on the caldron caused the mice to eat their way into the victim's abdomen; over crucifixion.

The number of executions has abated through the years. In thirty-one nations of the world and in thirteen states there are, legally, no more. No longer do we live in fear of being dragged off to execution for blasphemy, sodomy, bigamy, abortion, or any of sixty-four other capital offenses, as in eighteenth-century Sweden, and, in England, in the first quarter of the nineteenth century, for one or another of over two hundred offenses, among them coinage, fraudulent bankruptcy, horse theft, picking pockets, robbing a rabbit warren, associating with gypsies, damaging a fish pond, felling a tree. Although it is still the poor who are led to execution, they are not now put to death for the theft of a ruler, or two papers of nails, or two shillings and a counterfeit halfpenny. No longer are children hanged, as in England, far into the nineteenth century, when a boy of nine was sent to the gallows for breaking a shop window, a thirteen-year-old boy for stealing a spoon, and three children under eleven for stealing a pair of shoes; and no longer are mothers hanged for stealing to save their children from starvation. No longer do bodies hang in chains for months, and no longer are the heads of hanged and quartered persons parboiled by a humorous hangman with bay salt and cumin seed to preserve them for display about the city. No one now, except perhaps the prosecutor, holds a feast on the occasion of an execution, as did high officials of Newgate Gaol, while the several victims of the morning dangled together on the gallows and dense crowds of spectators filled the streets and debauches went on in rented rooms that overlooked the gallows. In Utah, now, no longer are there two hundred witnesses at a firing-squad execution; the law admits now only the sheriff, the prosecuting attorney, a representative from each news service, the physician, the county attorney, two ministers of the gospel, only as many peace officers as may be necessary, and five relatives or friends. Now those who witness executions anywhere are few and some faint at the sight and the witnessing for the many is done by newsmen whose job is to do the beholding for all and who may, someday, require the same namelessness and facelessness of the executioners.

The sky was dark at six in the evening, the moon up, with a rust-colored ring around it, but the sunlight was still on the high russet rocks behind the stores. They glowed in the darkness and a few clouds glowed in the dark sky and the snow glowed on the ground. The bus down from the north was boarded again by its torpid passengers. They filed out from the depot that was the lobby of a dismal hotel and out from the café off the lobby and down a narrow passageway to the bus waiting in the dimly lit lot at the back of the hotel. Among them were two sullen girls in jeans and white boots; a sailor; an old woman with bleached hair; and a young man who, settling in his seat again, muttered a curse against the state of Utah for its forbidding of smoking on buses.

There were no mountains and no deserts and no fertile fields in the darkness; far out glittered a small cluster of lights and a red light blinked above it. In the night, the wilderness of that high, cold plateau seemed of the years when the emigrant wagons, lining up in two rows with the trail between, established a town.

Every group going into the wilderness brought its own wilderness with it; along with the vision of God, along with the fierce strength that uprooted trees, broke hard earth, rerouted rivers, raised cities, every group escaping the superstitions of its oppressors brought its own superstitions with it, some belonging to those it escaped and some its very own, and in this wilderness we live still.

June 1966

Neal's Ashes

THE ASHES OF Neal Cassady are contained within a silver-gray rayon drawstring bag that fits within a crudely fancy box of varnished yellow wood shaped somewhat like a wedding cake on a platter, all of this weighing ten pounds on the bathroom scale of the woman who was his wife, the longest of three wives, in whose cupboard the ashes rest. Clutched in the arms of his last mistress, the ashes in their *Hecho en Mexico* box were conveyed back by bus from San Miguel where he was picked up unconscious beside the railroad tracks early one morning in 1968, a few days before his 42nd birthday. And all that *wild, yay-saying overburst of American joy,* in Kerouac's words, all that joy that he

embodied for the Beats and embodies now for the rock generation and for Sunday Supplement writers who have never, they
figure, experienced joy—who have only read of how it's experienced by somebody else and who overdose Cassady with joy—
was it so astoundingly there before the body was reduced to
ashes?

"I think he's happy here. He always wanted to come home."
Usually an offensive consolation that survivors parrot at grave-
sides, in this case it rings with the iron dolor of a bell in a
Mexican cathedral. The wife Carolyn is a little woman with the
fragility of body and the strength of mind that combine for an
evangelical endurance. Heather grows by the door; there's a
small lawn. The town is Los Gatos, a suburbia of ranch-style
houses an hour or so from San Francisco, on acreage that used to
be orchards. On the walls hang her pastel-toned oil paintings of
the three Cassady children, all now in their early 20s. On the coffee table and on the shelves and away in cupboards are some of
the novels and periodicals that contribute to the Neal Cassady
legend. She's writing her own story now.

"Allen came by to see the ashes and said he'd scatter them on
the Ganges if we liked, and then he said, 'Ask your son,' and John
said, 'What's the matter with them right here?' I was going to ask
Hugh Lynn Cayce if there was any place in the Cayce Foun-
dation where I could put them, because Neal was so wrapped
up in Cayce, but I didn't get to talk with him, he was so busy
last Saturday—all those people. I'd thought before about Unity,
because they have a practice of scattering them on their rose gar-
dens, but Neal wasn't Unity-sold. That teaching insists that you
think of yourself as part of God, and Neal just couldn't do it, and
every time I'd bring it up he'd get violent, he'd say 'I read all that
in prison.' As far as I know he loathed himself all the time. He
couldn't think of himself as good, an expression of God. All that,

even in the Cayce parts, he'd scourge. He didn't believe in a good God. He demanded proof, and to him the proof would be if God were stronger than his own will and his own desires. God could stop him, and then he would believe in Him."

Although the number of years of a marriage don't always add up to a greater knowledge of a mate, there was something to be gleaned from 16 years and from the five years after the divorce when "he hung around like a shadow." She knew him as well as any of the many others who claim now to have known him so well, and yet who are unable to suspect a dark side to any heavenly body.

"So many of the young men who are enamored of the Neal myth, they feel a longing to imitate him. Obviously the image has a response in everybody's longings, and Kerouac's. But if you get down to what it was in essence, like liberty or lack of restrictions or inhibitions or rules, whatever it is that Neal represented for them, like freedom and fearlessness, Neal was fearless but he wasn't free. Neal wanted to die. So he was utterly fearless as far as chances went because he was asking for it all the time. I kept thinking that the imitators never knew and don't know how miserable these men were, they think they were having marvelous times — joy, joy, joy — and they weren't at all."

It's not evident on her face or in her voice — the hard way she came to her knowledge of him. Rather, there's an attempt to make light of her experience as if she's still in the presence of very young children who must not be alarmed. He attempted suicide, he told her, a couple of times when he was in his teens.

"He said something about hiding under a bridge, I remember. I think he was going to drown himself. Then one day, back when we were living in San Francisco, he tried to do it with a gun. But I got the gun away from him and then he was ashamed of himself that he couldn't do it. But after that we ran into the Cayce thing about suicide and he wouldn't do it because of the penalty. There are as many different ways of paying for it as there are of doing it and motives for doing it, and some of the penalties that Cayce and other seers have mentioned — sometimes you spend a whole lifetime in frustration, sometimes you're killed right at the moment when you want to live the most. Because you misunderstood the value of life you must learn the value of life. He really took that to heart, but he got around it by sneaking around it. As long as his motive was not to destroy his life he felt he was conning God."

She gets up from the sofa to answer the phone. A social worker is calling about the 16-year-old runaway girl who has chosen to live with Carolyn, and the undertone of compassion in her low voice, as she talks on the phone, indicates who she was, for Cassady and for Kerouac, too, who spoke of her this way: *And I shudder sometimes to think of all that stellar mystery of how she is going to get me in a future lifetime, and I seriously do believe that will be my salvation, too. A long way to go.*

"I think they were trying to be something else to the other," she says of that famed comradeship. "Each one wanted the other to admire him. Jack, who was reticent, thought that Neal had this wonderful way of overcoming his own reticence and could just go ahead and sweep the women off their feet.

"Well, Neal never enjoyed it unless there was violence. He couldn't manage it any other way. The only times he was ever not able to do it was when I was offering or willing. It had to be rape. Until finally I only submitted because I was afraid of him. At last, then, I said, 'I can't stand it anymore, kill me or whatever,' and much to my surprise he was very nice about it, he seemed to understand. Of course, he had dozens on the outside anyway. Jack was very romantic and loving and not very good in bed, either. Apologetic. He was the other extreme. He felt he was doing something he shouldn't to a woman and I think that's why he preferred whores."

She was lover to Jack while married to Neal. "Neal wanted it that way. He always passed on his girlfriends to Jack, it was a ritual. It happened to me and I had to work it through. I knew about L———, Neal's first wife, that they'd shared her. In those days I thought she was a loose woman, that she didn't care who she slept with, and since they were all three traveling together . . . I didn't think of it as Neal's sharing, as Neal's idea. But then when Jack was living with us — Jack who was very, very moral, oddly enough, and so strait-laced about other people's wives — Neal was called to go on a two-week hold-down on the railroad and when he left he said, 'My best pal, my best gal' and Jack and I were just perfect all the time he was gone, we hardly dared to be in the same room together. When Neal came back I said, 'Did you say that because you were afraid we were going to and you didn't want to be made a fool of, or did you say it because you really wanted it to happen?' He said, 'Oh, I thought it would be nice.' So I said to myself, 'If that's how you are then let's see how nice it is.' Because he was really jealous and it was the only way I could keep him home. It worked like a charm. They both stayed home and watched each other. I had two husbands for a long time. It wasn't actually all that great as far as sex was concerned, there was nothing all that exciting in either one of them, but at least it made home life fun and we could all do things together where before they'd always gone out and I was left. Or like one time, before, when they brought home a couple of whores.

"Jack first lived with us in 1952 and wrote some of *On the Road* and *Visions of Cody.* Then he came back the next year and we'd moved to San Jose, and he lived with us six months and worked on the railroad. So he'd be out and Neal would be home and Neal would be out and Jack would be home. We had a big house with an extra bedroom and that was Neal's idea, we always had to have a room for Jack. And one reason why it all quit was that we bought this house and realized afterwards there was no place for Jack, and he was quite hurt because he'd sort of worked out his life that he'd spend six months with us and a month or so in Mexico and then he'd go back to see his mother and then he'd come out with us. And this house, as well as the fame and fortune, clobbered it — it all came at the same time. But they were thinking of putting a trailer in the backyard, it was just accepted that he'd live with us whenever he could. Of course, we were terribly discreet. Whenever Neal was around, Jack and I were perfectly proper. Even though Neal knew and offered this, he'd get fits of jealousy. But he seemed to like the idea, it was his way of showing Jack his love by sharing his women. No matter who it was he always offered her to Jack."

Whatever meanings are to be got from this giving, Kerouac in his novel about his breakdown, *Big Sur,* at last wonders why. He wonders in that novel about the possibility of envy and enmity in those friends he loved so well, and prefers to tell himself that he's lost his mind . . . *Gone the way of the last three years of drunken hopelessness which is a physical and spiritual and metaphysical hopelessness you can't learn in school no matter how many books on existentialism or pessimism you read, or how many jugs or vision-producing Ayahuasca you drink, or Mescaline take, or Peyote goop up with . . . The face of yourself you see in the mirror with its expression of unbearable anguish so haggered and awful with sorrow you can't even cry for a thing so ugly, so lost, no connection whatever with early perfection and therefore nothing to connect with tears or anything.* Yet the sedentary adulators of Cassady, comparing him with his compadre Kerouac who closeted himself away in a corner of the continent and drank himself to death, now write in their columns of Cassady that he "stayed on the road of Life, the

road of Kicks, the road of Now . . . always on top of everything,"
and disallowing him anything but joy they attribute his last days'
despondency, "if there had been any," only to the unavailability of
speed down there in San Miguel.

SHE MET NEAL shortly after the war, when she was enrolled at
the University of Denver. A mutual friend, a young man who fre-
quented the campus and the pool halls, brought Neal up to her
room. "The boy used to follow me around, always telling me
about these fantastic exploits of his that turned out to be Neal's.
So then he told me about Neal, he built up this great hero and I
was abashed, I idolized him before I met him. We lived together
a month and then he went off with Allen Ginsberg to Burroughs'
ranch in Texas where he was growing acres of pot. I couldn't
compete with that and came out to California. Allen has just sent
me a lot of letters that Neal wrote to him and they're passionate
love letters, but it looks like Neal was just leading him on. He
was down there in Texas for just a few days and he rejected Allen,
and Allen asked him for one last night but Neal got a girl, instead.

"Allen wrote a very poignant letter to Neal about that sad
night in a hotel room, it was his last night before he shipped out.
Years later, when we were in San Jose, Allen came to see us and
I found them making love . . . Neal was ambi to an extent. I think
it was just any kind of sex because it was such a masochistic
thing. He even got a kick out of allowing men to do it to him. He
didn't like men, didn't seek them, he just would let them once in
a while. Sex was his real devil, because he masturbated constantly if he wasn't with a woman, until in later years he preferred
it instead of hassling with a woman. But he loathed himself for it,
he did it to punish himself and every time he'd be nauseated.
Probably because of his Catholic beginnings he took the 'miserable worm' part to heart, he felt he was cursed with that need."

Yet someone else, a friend of the Cassadys', an elderly astrologer, likens him to a legendary figure called the Love Apple, a handsome man who gave of himself to all who desired him in order to assuage their human loneliness.

"When he got into spiritual counseling it was in the hope that somebody would give him an answer. What was interesting about the first tape of Past Lives readings — he had a horrendous experience, being castrated. By an enemy officer. He was in the Babylonian army, a general of Nebuchadnezzar, and he was in battle with a Hebrew army, but he fell for a girl and without thinking he made her and she happened to be the wife of a Hebrew officer, who caught him and publicly castrated him. So he never went back to his family but he became the vice king of Babylon in an effort to show that he could be as much a man or as powerful as any. He became the chief of the underworld and mostly in violent things like bullfighting and bear baiting. And if that reading was true it seemed to tie in with the compulsion."

Not many people break their thumbs and it is likely that those thumbs that do get broken heal without complications. Cassady's bandaged thumb that is granted a long paragraph in *On the Road* was not without heavy consequences unknown to Kerouac.

"He hit his first wife on the forehead and broke his thumb. He was up in her hotel room and she wanted to be rid of him, she was waiting for her fiancé to get off a ship any day. Then he came back to me and I drove him to the hospital and he couldn't do any work. It had this cast with a big traction hook because a thumb is particularly hard to set. So I let him take care of Cathy, who was four months old, and I went to work. Well, we had this crummy place on Liberty Street and he had to wash diapers in the sink and he probably wrang them with that hand and got urine in it. Then he went back to changing tires before it was healed, and he always drove himself so hard and fast, he not only had to be the best and the most amazing worker, but it was like flagellation, and the cast was just mash. The bone got infected and I had to give him penicillin shots, but he left for New York and in the end they had to cut off the tip of his thumb.

"And later on, more than ten years later, the same medium who gave us the Past Lives readings was doing a thing she'd invented on the theory that the thumb print is directly connected with the pituitary gland. She'd done these fantastic experiments, printing the thumb print on some kind of crystal stuff, and she made photographic slides and got these amazing color patterns —each print is like an aura. Neal wanted one done and then we realized that the thumb print on his dominant hand was amputated. It seemed spooky to him because his connection with the pituitary, which occultly is like the highest mind, was shot. It seemed terribly significant, it meant that he had been crippled in the spiritual realm."

No matter how many persons engage in the attempt to divulge and delineate a particular person, it seems an impossibility to know, at last, that chosen one. The mystery only deepens. "Neal was known as a woman beater. He couldn't stay with one woman and some of them couldn't be true to one man and so they tortured him in the same way. N——— was paranoid. She threatened to kill herself and it looks as if she did—she slipped off a roof trying to get away from the police, but she'd already cut her throat with a piece of glass from a broken skylight. That's the kind of girl he took up with.

"They lost $10,000 on the races, it was part of what we got for that accident when he was working on the railroad, he fell off a boxcar and mangled his foot. Some of the money went to buy this house and the rest went down the drain. She forged my signature . . . It doesn't diminish from the man any, from the goodness of him, because the thing that appealed to people was his enormous kindness and compassion. I was impressed with his standards which were true Christian standards that everybody else put down. In other words, I always felt deeply that he had ideals that were stronger than most men's, than sterling citizens'. He had convictions and beliefs that were bigger than the social values. He couldn't do those values at all, but the deep down spiritual values . . . He could talk and would talk with anybody and instantly they felt that he really cared about them. How many people do you know who give of their whole selves when you first meet them? And it was a powerful thing because he was so perceptive and intelligent that he could meet them right where they were. Now part of that became conning, he learned how to use that to con. He was a master at getting you to think that he knew exactly where you were and what you needed and he could always supply it."

THE GENTLE WOMAN in the old sweater goes relentlessly on until you wonder if that legendary figure behind the wheel of the Merry Pranksters' bus — the man who they like to claim knew intuitively that the way was clear when he went around curves on the wrong side of the highway — wasn't the driver after all but some unnameable stranger they'd picked up, out there in the night.

"Before the bus trip he threw himself down and burst into tears. He couldn't stand himself and the life he was living. He couldn't drop everybody but he resolved that when he was with them he wouldn't be the clown anymore. But they'd all stand around and expect him to perform and he couldn't help it, he'd start off again and then he'd be lost. Everybody could recognize the brilliance of his mind but you simply couldn't stay with it, your mind couldn't work that fast. It was astonishing the way his mind worked but it drove you crazy. He'd take more and more drugs to keep it up and be what they expected him to be. I don't know whether they thought he was a sage or just weird. I used to think that they exploited him but I don't think so now. He liked doing it, it was an ego boost when people wanted him to perform. But he got sick of himself. Near the end he was at Kesey's farm in Oregon, and I guess it was in the middle of a big party and Neal couldn't stand it another minute and he rushed out without a jacket, without his cigarettes, and went to the highway and hitchhiked down and called me from a friend's house in Larkspur. They'd put him to bed, he'd collapsed. I got Al Hinkle to drive me up, and on the way home Neal was hanging on to my hand. I was in the front seat and he was lying on the back seat. He said he couldn't stand another minute the way he was living. Al talked to him about a job on the railroad again, he said the administration had changed and that maybe they'd be more sympathetic.

"Neal knew all along, I'm sure, that he couldn't do it but he was going along with it because there was nothing else to do. And when Al went home Neal started racing up and down the hallway. He'd throw himself on his knees by John's bed and rock and moan and groan and when I'd try to comfort him he'd say, 'No, it's all right,' and I'd back off and come in here and sit because I didn't know what was going to happen next, and he came racing in here. 'Where's John? Where's John? I killed my son. I killed my son.' He said he had to wash his hair or take a shower and I could hear the water running but he was pounding on the walls and yelling and I was terrified. Then he calmed down and came out and sat at the table and opened his Bible which he carried with him all the time and started reading a passage which I can't find again, but it was something about bad companions. Then in a minute or two he went to bed and I thought he was dead.

"We were into Past Lives readings a lot and in a past life with

John he was responsible for his son's being chopped up by knife blades on chariot wheels. They were both charioteers in Assyria, or somewhere, and Neal had invented knife blades for the wheels, for warfare, but the blades were on when they were racing, and John looked back and saw that Neal was losing his balance and they both fell and both died, but Neal, as he died, watched his son cut to ribbons. We thought we'd never find anybody like Cayce, never anybody that good. There's this old lady in San Jose who's in touch with all these people, she has a big house and most of them stay there when they come to town, like the Cayce people, and she always kept us in touch with them. Then in 1963, I guess it was, this woman came to town. She was a medium, they call them channels now. She was supposedly a channel for a Seventh Plane Astral Teacher. She traveled around the country and gave Past Lives readings, so by the time we got to her there were a lot of tapes of other people's that we could hear and see whether we were interested, and the tapes were fantastic. They could have been made up and we weren't positive they were all gospel truth but we figured if those things hadn't happened then something very much like them must have, because we got a lot of vibes.

"She turns on the tape recorder and goes into a trance and the spirit guide, the person who's passed on to the other side, takes over and through her he gives you the lives that he feels relate to this one. Now the first tape you got, the first year, was supposed to be the physical and emotional lives, then the next year it was spiritual karma and another set of lives. And Neal's first reading was just awful. You never heard of such ghastly lives, they made this one look like a picnic. I'm sure they couldn't give everybody that information, not everybody could stand it. He ended up sobbing at the end of it, he was really broken up. That's the only thing I can connect that night with. He might have lived that life, he might have had some memory, but he always felt guilty about John, that he wasn't the father he would like to have been."

Was he in triple binds, then—the binds of the Self, and over that the binds of somebody else's image of him in literature, an exaggeration he had to live up to, and over that the binds laid upon him by some spirit guide on the Other Side—the task of working off some mistakes and mishaps in previous existences?

"And in the morning he got up early, he went with a railroad conductor who was going to drive him to San Francisco to get his job back. He played the whole scene perfectly sanely, like he was going to do it, and he was going to come back that night and start all over. Everything was going to be great, you know. Then for two weeks we never knew what happened, we didn't hear a word, and then the kids saw him in the city, on a bus. They said he'd been arrested and been in jail for all the warrants out against him for driving without a license. Periodically at this point he was getting caught and if his friends didn't have the money to pay the fine he'd go to jail for the weekend or a week. His mind was gone. Jamie said he didn't recognize her, he kept talking to her girl friend as if she were Jamie. I didn't see much of him after that. Once or twice . . .

"HE'D BEEN GOING around with a girl, J———, in San Francisco, and she was urging Neal to go to Mexico and get well and write, etcetera. People say they quarreled terribly. The odd thing about her was that she heard voices and they told her he was going to be all well in six weeks. She said she could heal him, she said she had this house there. She was the daughter of a wealthy family in Philadelphia. I kept urging him to do it because of the warrants and I thought that maybe in the sun and quiet possibly he'd get well. He looked awful. She wrote to me when he died, and letters after, telling me about what transpired, but she gave me a couple of different versions and she was talking more and more in her letters about psychic phenomena, like each time she looked in the mirror she saw his face. She was strung out on drugs. He was in San Miguel only a couple of days and the last night he went to this wedding. He was on seconal all day and he didn't drink as a rule but he drank at the wedding. Whether he did it carelessly or whether he knew what he was doing, nobody will ever know. The only thing that came of the autopsy was that the contents of the stomach had an alcoholic smell and everything was congested. It seems to have been the combination of seconal and alcohol, and he was already sick from speed.

"Of course, Hugh Lynn Cayce told him he would never be allowed out through suicide and he knew that himself, just from his own feelings — that he had this hard thing to do and he was going to have to live it. So you see, that's why I don't know about that last minute. I knew how he felt about suicide and yet his mind was so gone and he could have got to the point where he just couldn't stand it, and that was stronger than his belief about suicide. Or more likely, I feel that he just kind of went to hell and didn't care. Risked it. In other words, he may have felt that since he'd been risking his life all along he might just as well take the drinks on a dare, and it worked this time. Not to purposely end it, because he may have felt that even *that* was going to be denied him. I know how desperate he was, he called me from Los Angeles before he went down to Mexico and said he was coming home. He kept saying, 'I'm coming home, I'm coming home,' on and on. So I know he was miserable. There was no place to go, no place to turn, and he said, 'Well, maybe by my birthday,' and I didn't hear the rest of the sentence.

"So she brought the ashes all the way up, hugging them in her arms, on the bus, and got across the border. When she came here she didn't want to let them out of her arms, so first I just put them on a table, here, for that evening — she came at night — and when she went to bed I stashed them. She was so strange, she hung around all day. I painted and she sat beside me and rapped and then she'd start singing and then she'd break into laughter. She turned up at the door again a week later, she wanted to see the ashes and say goodbye. I guess she was hitchhiking."

Of the several women who were his wives and mistresses and who remain in touch with Carolyn, only one has a share of the ashes — the woman he lived with after he and Kerouac left for New York in that time, more than 20 years ago, of the bandaged thumb, when Cathy was still an infant and Carolyn was pregnant with Jamie.

"She asked me if I'd get a divorce and I said if Neal will ask me. She wrote the letter and he signed it, and that hurt, too. She got pregnant and he did his duty. He went to Mexico for a quick divorce and then he married her, but he left the same day to come back here. I think he married her bigamously, I never got the divorce papers. Both other marriages were annulled, the first and that one, the third. She thought I ought to split the ashes with her and I finally gave her a teaspoonful. I said, 'You knew him for one year and I've known him for twenty.' I put them in a little box and wrapped it in foil and she said they arrived on her husband's birthday, and her daughter by that marriage put them at her father's place at dinner, thinking it was a birthday package for him. She thought that was terribly funny.

"She'd call me up and tell me what she was going to do with them, she had all these ideas. First she was going to put them in her family plot in New Hampshire, then she called to say, 'Do you think I ought to buy a tree in Washington Square?' Then she said 'You know what I'm going to put with them? You remember that quarter that has an eagle on it, one way it's an eagle and the other way it looks like a cowboy with a hardon? Don't you think that would be appropriate to put with the ashes?'

"Then I didn't hear from her for a while and finally she called and said she'd phoned Stella Kerouac, Jack's widow, in Florida, who'd never heard of her, and asked if she'd let her bury the ashes on Jack's heart. That was *it*. So Stella told her that when she sold the house in Florida she and Jack's mother were going back to Lowell and that she hadn't got Jack a proper headstone yet and when she did she'd meet her there and they could dig up the grave."

She brings out the fancy box containing the ashes and sets it on the coffee table. Stapled to a side of the box is a scrap of paper on which is typed *Contiene Cenizas Del Sr. Neal Cassady Jr.* in faint ink.

October 12, 1972

WATCHED:
The New Student President

ON THE NIGHT of October 20, 1966, twenty masked Delta Tau Delta men surrounded their student body president on a street of the Stanford campus, escorted him to an empty lot and, with electric clippers plugged into an outlet inside a dormitory, shaved off the abundant hair of his head. "They expected me to fight back," Harris recalled when I spoke to him about the incident. "I figured I had a captive audience so I had a fifteen-minute conversation with this guy with a wolf mask who was holding my right leg — talking about education. After they shaved my head I said, 'Look, I've cooperated with you so far so we'll make a deal

—you spare my beard.' And they did, after a big debate. I had to
go to Michigan the next week and it was freezing cold."

Fraternity men find themselves confused by changing times.
If those masked twenty were laboring under the biblical superstition that when the locks are shorn the strength ebbs they must
have been surprised to learn that the strength increased. Or if
the assault was a diversionary tactic, an attempt to make the
issue the length of their adversary's hair because the real issue
was even more intolerable—changing times—one, at least,
among them, traced and questioned by a reporter from *The
Stanford Daily*, admitted some degree of self-probing: "Harris
really showed the Delts a lot of class. He made us feel sorry we
did it." It was his way of conceding that the men, bearded or
unbearded, elected these days to the presidency of the student
body in more universities than a few may be men of courage and
conscience.

Students in these changing times are challenging the arbiters
of the academy and of the hierarchical regions above and beyond.
Within the past year or so several dignitaries have been met on
the campuses by large and vociferous demonstrations. At Stanford, Vice-President Hubert Humphrey, emerging from the audi-
torium into his protective wedge of police and Secret Service
men, ran for his car to escape some thousand angry students;
Defense Secretary Robert S. McNamara was forced from his car
—a police wagon—and onto the hood of another car by eight
hundred Harvard students who wanted to ask him a few questions before he left the campus; while students at Berkeley, some
silently, some not, greeted U.N. Ambassador Arthur Goldberg
with picket signs and a walkout by five hundred persons when
that gentleman came by to pick up an honorary degree. A solid
wall of one hundred fifty students blockaded the Chancellor of
the University of Wisconsin in his office until he wrote the check

that bailed out eighteen students arrested earlier for demonstrating against the campus-recruitment campaign of the Dow Chemical Company, manufacturers of napalm. At the University of Michigan, the Student Council lifted itself right out of the administrative Office of Student Affairs after administrators, during summer vacation when most students were away, handed over to the House Un-American Activities Committee the membership lists of student organizations opposed to the war in Vietnam. And so it follows that the men elected to student offices now, at universities around the country, are not keepers of those sacred flames of ritual and protocol and administrative decree.

Columbia's David Langsam, Cornell's David Brandt, Berkeley's Dan McIntosh, Amherst's Steve Cohen, San Francisco State's Jim Nixon, University of Minnesota's Howie Kaibel, University of North Carolina's Robert Powell, University of Houston's Richard Gaghagen, University of Michigan's Ed Robinson range from the "thoughtful middle," as distinguished from the old unthinking middle, to the Far Left, and their force has been felt in everything from the structuring of the new experimental colleges within the universities to the refusal by several university administrations to comply with the ranking mechanism of Selective Service. And among these leaders, David Harris — the young man tackled by the twenty old guards — is the one most often cited by student editors and other presidents. "He gathers disciples around him wherever he goes," said one disciple, and since he has spoken at so many campuses across the country he has gathered quite a number.

After meeting Harris for the first time at the 1966 National Student Association Congress at the University of Illinois, Neil Reichline, editor of the *U.S.L.A. Daily Bruin,* kept his staff up night after night to discuss Harris' ideas on education, and through the pages of the *Bruin* brought about a great surge of interest in reform. "I was confronted by him and he blew my mind," Reichline recalls. "Dave's views on educational reform, on the Vietnam war, on the draft, are not based on political expediency. They follow naturally from his life-style, his mentality. His concern for his 'soul,' for his values, and for himself as a valuable person are manifested in his concern for the communities that he exists in, whether they are his school, city, or nation. He confronts you with this mentality, this concern for community, and you just can't pass over it without some self-examination, some thought on your role as a human being and how you're going to relate to other human beings. You can't meet Dave Harris and not change your life in some way." Ed Robinson, the president who cut the cord between the student government and the administration at the University of Michigan, describes him this way: "Not only is Harris intelligent, he takes the next step and applies that intelligence to thinking about his surroundings, and then he takes another step and draws some conclusions, and then he takes the farthest step and acts on the basis of those conclusions. In this step-by-step progress we fall down somewhere, most of us." The students are not alone: David Harris was one of several persons invited to participate in a meeting on students and the draft, called by Kingman Brewster, President of Yale. And in the editorial offices of *The Stanford Daily,* a file card, on the wall for months after David's resignation, read: "I don't know what Dave's reasons are for resigning and maybe that's beside the point. His A.S.S.U. administration has taken its toll on him and, I think in the long run beneficially, on official Stanford. But he's been there long enough for all of us to see his real stature, his authentic qualities of greatness. How often do you see a man who, in being himself, can help you be and find yourself; in whom you're able to detect no deviousness at all; whose compassion is no less compassionate for being unsentimental; who cares like hell about the world he lives in and can somehow go on loving and believing in the people who inhabit it, even while he protests the ways we go on lousing it up? For all his sharp, unremitting criticism — in part, of course, because of it — all of us, and all of Stanford, and the whole college and university scene in America are better for having him where he's been." The card was signed B. Davie Napier, Dean of the Chapel and Professor of Religion.

ON THE FRONT door of the pale-green shingle house in the Negro neighborhood of East Palo Alto hung a penciled sign reading: Go Around to the Back Door. (His study room is in the back of the house, I learned a few minutes later, and if any other tenant of the house had been playing a record loudly, my knock would have gone unheard.) He opened the front door anyway, because two neighbor children, roaming in and out, saw me from an upstairs window as I made my way through the high grass; I heard them calling to him. He is a tall and strong-bodied young man with thick, blond hair, sideburns — the beard is gone, he shaved it off one day for whatever significant or insignificant reason — pale blue eyes, rimless glasses, and a substantial moustache that makes him appear a few years older than his twenty-one. He had interrupted his part-time job at Kepler's bookstore, owned by a prominent pacifist, to meet me. On the bright yellow wall of the living room hung a large photo of Charlie Chaplin with cane and derby, and a restaurant stove took up a good part of the floor space, a relic of the time Harris and the other tenants of the house were implementing plans — failed ones — to open a small café in Palo Alto. The window of his study looked out on a huge, fallen tree, an old blue bus with flowered curtains, serving as bedroom for one of the students of that communal house, and more high grass. The two neighbor boys, grammar-school age and loud talkers, gazed in from the hallway until they were asked to close the door. Out in another room a Bob Dylan record began and someone shouted from the kitchen, "The water's boiling!" An old suede jacket, mended carefully in a dozen places, hung from the closet door, boots were strewn on the floor, and a mother cat and four kittens lay atop a soft pile of clothes in a corner of the open closet.

The young man in the sagging, upholstered chair under the small photograph of Gandhi was scheduled to address in four days a massive peace mobilization in San Francisco. A senior, one of five students majoring in Social Thought among thirty in the Honors Program, an independent study program for self-motivated students, he was also teaching a class at the Free University of Palo Alto called "A Life of Peace and Liberation in the U.S." Ashes fell from his cigarette into the crevices of the chair — his fingers are nicotine stained down to the middle knuckles — and as we talked books slid from the chair's wide curved arms. On the windowsill and on the shelf were Nietzsche, Kierkegaard, A.J. Muste, the Upanishads. I asked him about his use of the I Ching, the ancient Chinese Book of Changes.

"We never just open it and read it like a book," he said. "We treat it like a friend around here. We treat it like a living thing." Would he turn to it before his speech? To oblige me he turned to it then, first tossing three Chinese coins onto the rug six times. The result of this encounter with chance led him to the hexagram that in turn directed him to a page of the text:

"The weight of the great is excessive. The load is too heavy for the strength of the supports. . . . It is an exceptional time and situation; Therefore extraordinary measures are demanded. It is necessary to find a way of transition as quickly as possible, and to take action. This promises success. For although the strong element is in excess, it is in the middle, that is, at the center of gravity, so that a revolution is not to be feared. Nothing is to be achieved by forcible measures. The problem must be solved by gentle penetration to the meaning of the situation. . . . Then the changeover to other conditions will be successful. It demands real superiority; therefore the time when the great preponderates is a momentous time."

"It's like taking a sighting off the top of a wave," he explained. "It gives you a sense of the forces of life around you and finds your relationship to those forces for that moment."

His heavy build, Levis and sideburns suggest a farm laborer in the town of Fresno, California, where he grew up, the son of an attorney, and worked in the packing sheds; or they suggest a figure in an old labor photograph of the West, posing by dray horses and by timber. "He used to wear a big buckle on his belt," one of his friends was later to tell me, "and when he spoke he was always shifting it up because his Levis were over-washed and were faded out to grey." He probably resembles his grandfathers and probably hopes that he does. One was a wood craftsman in Fresno—"I go over to his workshop—he's dead now but his workshop is still there—and pick up scraps of what he'd been doing. I have a goblet he made on a lathe, the walls of the wood are thin as glass—all out of one piece." The other grandfather worked in the open-pit copper mines in Utah. He talks with a fast mixture of beat jargon, academic terms, and words in common usage, and there is an accent that's Southwest, the rural parts.

Up to a few years ago a university for the offspring of California aristocracy, Stanford—its arcaded yellow stone buildings on an almost unbelievable number of acres of thick grass, oaks, and date palms—now has endowment funds sufficient to grant scholarships to the sons and daughters of the less affluent, and Harris is one of these recipients. When he came to Stanford in 1963 he was, according to his own description, an all-American frosh type, a state finalist in competitive speech from Fresno

High who made innocuous speeches of no content, and a three-year veteran on the football team. Mississippi hit in that year, and the freshman dormitory at Stanford became a communication center for the South. In the Fall of 1964, in his sophomore year, he went South with a carload of Stanford students. With four others he entered Quitman County, Northwest Mississippi, wilderness territory. Their lives were constantly threatened and one of that group was kidnapped and beaten. "Essentially, when I was in Mississippi it wasn't as big a thing as when I got back, because when I got back I really started thinking about what I'd done there. Mississippi blew my mind. From there I got involved in the whole anti-war activity, from there it was a natural educational progression. The South wasn't just a boil on the face of America. The hate and brutality there were indigenous to the way America lives."

At evening programs on the campus he spoke about Mississippi, he spoke against the draft, against the war in Vietnam, and he criticized the educational system at Stanford. "It's all one thing. Once someone gets involved in Peace there's no turning back from it, it's a style of life, not something considered politics removed from one. It makes dealing with others a very direct expression of one's being." In his junior year he was approached by a group of students to run for president of the student body. He agreed to run in order to force the other candidates to face the issues, but he preferred to lose. He won, in the largest balloting in Stanford's history. "The platform was a long list of changes based on the attitude that Stanford is not educating and has no understanding of what education is. Students have no right of control over their own lives. It's a system calculated on the impotence of the students in that it makes everything the student does something outside himself. What that does is teach people to be powerless. We started from the initial statement that education is something that happens in your mind, the mind learning itself, learning how to use itself. It's a very inner process and the function that teachers traditionally serve in most of the cultures of the world—where they haven't gotten to modern industrial teaching which is essentially a training mechanism— is one of spiritual guidance. Not only should a teacher know things but he should have an understanding, a wisdom about things, beyond simply knowing them. So that a teacher provides himself as a mirror to the other person's mind and gives that person a glimpse into his own mind so he can then start educating himself. That's what education is and it isn't this whole social system at Stanford, the superficialities. They rigidify the students here into cogs for the great American wheel. Most people who teach at colleges are doing it for very simple security reasons and they don't like people to rock the boat even though they make a big thing about intellectual inquiry and all that. A professor will allow you to put down the administration but will get offended if you say the faculty is irrelevant, which they are, by and large, except for maybe ten people, and they're relevant as people because they've developed a style of living that really has relevance to other lives. Then we talked about who runs the universities, that they shouldn't belong to the trustees because they should belong to the people who are really involved in the spiritual process of learning, they should belong to the students and anyone who wants to enter into it." One of the other planks of the platform was the abolition of fraternities. "It's all one thing." Nothing is separable from the rest.

After his election, Harris met for the first time with J.E. Wallace Sterling, President of Stanford. He went into the latter's office with beard, work shirt, Levis, and moccasins. "He has a smooth way of dealing with people," Harris told me. "He never made it clear to me that he might have been dismayed by me."

As president of the student body, Harris led a Stanford dele-
gation to the National Student Association Congress and proposed to the liberal caucus — roughly about one half of the five
hundred people there — a resolution calling for immediate with-
drawal of U.S. troops from Vietnam. Debate in the caucus lasted
until four-thirty in the morning. The resolution failed; the one
that passed the caucus and eventually the Congress called for a
cease-fire and negotiations, and drew this comment from Harris:
"If you come out with this resolution, you will be saying that you
feel strongly about the war but you don't want to say it." Another
resolution proposed by Harris, calling for abolition of the draft
and formation of a draft-resistance movement, was also softened
by the liberal caucus and passed by the Congress. After some
"soul sessions" a radical caucus was formed and walked out on
the liberal caucus. For liberals Harris has no favorable word.
"They recite all the American virtues — 'We are loyal American
citizens who believe in America, La de da de da de da. . . .' They
fall on their knees to President Johnson and say, 'Please reconsider, there may be something wrong with the war.' That way of
doing things — bribing people, getting to their egos, all kinds of
insidious things. What they're doing is further entrenching the
whole attitude that brought this war about." On the N.S.A., in
particular: "The only time members ever get together is for that
Congress where they pass policy declarations and nobody does
anything about them. The rest of the time it's run by a kind of oli-
garchic bureaucracy. Most of the people who go to N.S.A. and
involve themselves look upon themselves as future Congress-
men and Senators."

At the end of February 1967, Harris resigned from the presidency of the Stanford student body. "The job had become a trap
for my mind," he explained to me. "I'd done my bit for education,
I'd given over two hundred speeches at Stanford and was repeat-

ing myself. I'd lost real communication with students because they treated me like a famous figure, they'd just sit and watch me do it and weren't putting themselves on the line." Another reason he gave at the time of resignation was: "My contribution has basically been to say things to the community that up to this point the community was afraid to say to itself. I was just a spokesman for a basic way of seeing the university that I felt had to be articulated if there was going to be any healthy notion of education."

I asked him to name the literature that was most meaningful for him. The list was long, including "almost every religious document," among them the Buddhist scriptures, the Bible, Lao-Tzu's *The Way of Life,* Gandhi, Jung, Fromm, Marcuse, Marx, as sociologist rather than economist, Cassirer. Of the novelists — Faulkner, Joyce, Conrad, and of the poets — Tagore, Lorca. "They all come closer to understanding man than anyone else, in their own unique fashion." He writes poetry himself and some of it has been used in a poetry class that another of the student-tenants, Bill Shurtleff, teaches in the garage, where he also sleeps. A small volume of the combined poetry of Jeffrey Shurtleff, an honor student in the humanities, and David Harris is being put together within a cover designed for it by the photographers of the group, students Lary Goldsmith and Otto Schatz; the name given this enterprise — The Peace and Liberation Commune Press.

Harris came to his decision about the draft alone. He belongs to no organization, only the one he and some other students at Stanford and Berkeley have founded — the Bay Area Organizing Committee for Draft Resistance. His first step against the draft was his participation in the sit-in in President Sterling's office, protesting Stanford's acceptance of draft tests. "Student defer-ments are immoral," he said at that time. "They weed out the people who can afford an education." In June 1966, he sent back his student deferment, intending to apply for a conscientious-objector status, but not on a religious basis. A few months after he gave up his deferment, he made his decision about the draft, alone one summer night in his study. "I was just sitting there when all of a sudden, just out of the back of my mind, came the statement: Well, you're not going to cooperate with them. My first thought about jail really frightened me, I'd never thought about going to jail for a principle against the draft. But from then on I knew what my principle was. I sent them a letter, then, saying I believed myself to be more of a conscientious objector than the law allows because I didn't believe in the law. I said I was going to break that law. The law is immoral and there's no being moral within an immoral law."

Reclassified 1A, Harris took his pre-induction physical in his hometown, Fresno. "I knew I wasn't going to go along with them, but I wanted to see what they did, who went into the Army. I got to the last table and the doctor there said, 'Hey, Mac, this is this guy Harris, he's the guy who's going to refuse.'" Harris was informed by mail that he was fit; a month later he was informed that he was not. The board had changed its mind, classifying him 1Y—temporary physical or psychological disability—until September 1967, at which time it will reconsider classifying him back to 1A and Harris will fail to honor the directive to appear for another physical. "What I think about Peace in my own mind, how fully I'm understanding it, helps the growth of Peace in the world. In that sense what I'm doing is a very religious thing. I can't go out and talk about Peace if I don't feel in my own mind that I'm living it as fully as I can. So it's simply a question for me of keeping my own sense of integrity, which is what allows me to do all this against the war and against American society as it is now. It's essentially my own feeling of integrity. I think that any

movement is better for the fact that the people in it are following
their highest understanding, and if that means going to jail . . . I
feel that I couldn't talk about the draft if I wasn't out in a position
facing jail. We have an obligation to speak to the people of the
United States, and the act of going to prison is itself a statement
and a much more powerful one to the American consciousness
than taking a C.O. or going to Canada. I have a basic hang-up
about being run out of any place. I was run out of too many
places in Mississippi."

I asked him if he had his speech prepared for the mobilization
on Saturday. He said that he never prepared speeches. "I don't
speak about anything that has no relevance to my life. I usually
meditate before I speak. You get your mind down to a single
point, a pinpoint, and when you reach the pinpoint you go
through and come out clean, everything starts opening up and
filling out, a fresh vision of everything. In speaking, I try to get to
that pinpoint and then I get up and speak. Two years ago meditation was far from my life. I developed it from more and more
contact with Eastern thinking, Eastern music. They have a
whole different rhythm to their thinking, a much slower, a more
cyclical kind of rhythm, and my life just started getting into that
kind of rhythm. I'm calmer now, I used to get frenzied. Everything that happens isn't earth-shaking. It's like a quantum jump,
you break through into a new world. I think there's a danger,
though, in the American, the Western, reaction to Eastern thinking. They try to make themselves Easterners, which to my mind
is illegitimate. You can't run around being an Indian if you're an
American, you're not part of that culture. You go to the Haight-
Ashbury, it's all very speeded up, very hectic, which is the exact
opposite of what I associate with Eastern thinking. I'm not saying you can't learn from it, but what they take is the rote form and
they think they've reached Eastern thought when all they've got

are the cultural mechanisms. American society understands life in terms of fetishes and can only understand the spirit as a fetish. The people of Haight-Ashbury should ask themselves how much of what they're doing is fetish ridden. Then the culture there is organized around drugs and I think drugs are not a spiritual vortex. There's a great danger in their seeing things in terms of drugs. Love exists regardless of acid. Drugs can be useful but the nature of that activity is a minimal one. Acid stands knee-high to Peace. The son of a British Prime Minister—about a month before he died of an overdose of heroin he was talking to some friends about shooting smack and he said, 'At Cambridge everything is just around the corner. But when you go into your room and tie-off and shoot-up, everything is right there in your lap.' The real problem is how you can make a culture that's right there in someone's lap."

He talked about the war in Vietnam: "Johnson is having a hard time holding the whole thing together. I think his next move is a big escalation, invade Laos and Thailand and Cambodia and North Vietnam, and to do that he's going to have to double his manpower there and that's when the big climax is going to come, because all those people who are on student deferments are going to get called. If they escalate, there's not going to be a student deferment for anybody except engineers and medical students, and all those people in school now are going to be faced with that question by next year. He's going to try doing it first without being repressive, then he's going to get this opposition from the youth and he'll try to clamp down. The chances of anybody saying the kind of things we're saying now in a year—they'll harass you and bust you. That is, if you start getting people, and it's clear we're starting to get people."

He is positive their phone is tapped. "I know from Mississippi how it sounds, anything can foul up your phone when they put a tap in. In Mississippi we could hear the sheriff moving around in his office. I don't know who they're tapping for — one of the guys who lives here was subpoenaed by H.U.A.C. last summer in Washington for organizing that Stanford blood drive for the North Vietnamese civilians and I'm doing my Peace thing. They interrogated me when I came back from Mississippi because I was saying things about an agent back there who called me a nigger lover. They're meticulous. Every time we have a rally at Stanford there's always an F.B.I. agent there with his camera, with telescopic lens, taking pictures of everybody."

On Saturday morning, April 15, the marchers gathered at the foot of Market Street, filling up all the side streets for blocks, and when I found David Harris he was with his friends from Stanford and Berkeley, handing out, each from an armload, the Draft Resistance Committee's "We Refuse to Serve" declarations. By the time the students, numbering one-half to two-thirds of the 65,000 marchers, got started, the head of the procession had already reached Kezar Stadium, four miles away. Long hair and beards, if not the rule, were common in that massive contingent, along with fringed buckskin boots and the heavy kind, sheepskin vests, massed strings of beads. The placard, AMERICA, GO BACK, YOU'RE GOING THE WRONG WAY, may have verbalized one meaning, at least, of the costumes: they were out of the West of the last century, of a time before this country went that wrong way — if any reckoning can be made of the time when any country took that turn — and the new frontier these students were advocating was way out beyond the one the late President gave that name to. The rest of the world was no territory for a General by the Dr. Strangelove name of West! More Land! but a great frontier for the spirit. The fragrance of incense sticks drifted through the air that was sometimes misty, sometimes clear and warm, and the

Eye of God, the diamond-shaped colored-yarn symbol the Mexican Indians carry through their fields, was carried here down the main street. I saw Harris first on one corner, then another as he moved along between the students and the spectators. He was usually findable, being taller than most, but sometimes obscured by the placards and banners.

From a high-sided truck, Country Joe and the Fish, with beards, sheepskin vests, shoulder-length hair, a fur cap on one, and green peace signs painted on their cheeks, rolled out a tremendous rock dirge that set an hypnotic, solemn pace for the mass of students and resounded against the grey facades down the side streets and up Market Street and against the nudie movie where life-size cutouts of a soldier and marine were up on the marquee along with, "This is U.S. Servicemen Appreciation Week," and where *A Good Time with a Bad Girl* was showing. Further along the way, out near the stadium, musical accompaniment was furnished by three young men beating pots and pans up on a sixth-floor balcony and by a Bob Dylan record blaring full volume out of wide-open apartment windows where two elderly women sat with their elbows on the sills, and by a girl serenely sitting on a concrete wall and singing in a high, clear voice "Krishna . . . Hari."

By the time Harris reached the stadium most of the marchers were already in the bleachers and the speakers assembled on the platform out in the center of the green oval field. With him up there were Mrs. Martin Luther King, Julian Bond, the Georgia legislator, Robert Vaughn, the Man from U.N.C.L.E., Judy Collins, several clergymen, others. He was the only one in Levis and Levi jacket. He spoke very little to those on either side of him, then not at all as he began his meditation. While the others rose and spoke to the filled stadium, their voices blaring out in several directions through the clusters of red loudspeakers on the field, I saw him bend his head to his knees for a time. When I looked again he was sitting upright, his legs crossed, and one foot shaking restlessly.

Country Joe and the Fish, out of their truck and down on the track, struck up with electric organ, guitars, and voice their *I-Feel-Like-I'm-Fixin'-to-Die Rag,* familiar to students since the early Vietnam march in Berkeley in 1965 that was halted at the Oakland border by a line of helmeted police. On the track before them a crowd gathered and couples danced to that ragtime mockery of wartime acquiescence.

> Come on all of you big strong men;
> Uncle Sam needs your help again.
> He's got himself in a terrible jam;
> Way down yonder in Vietnam.
> So put down your books and pick up a gun;
> We're gonna have a whole lot'a fun.
> 'Cause it's one, two, three, "What are we fighting for?"
> "Don't ask me I don't give a damn";
> Next Stop is Vietnam
> And it's five, six, seven, open up the pearly gates
> There ain't no time to wonder why,
> Whoopie! We're all gonna die!

Just before Harris began to speak, down across the field and into the parking lot out of sight behind the stadium wall drifted a black-clad parachutist from an unseen source, his white and black and yellow chute inscribed with the word LOVE.

Harris loomed over the microphone, his face and voice impassioned: "We have to realize we're mistaken if we call this war Johnson's war or if we call this war the Congress' war. This war is a logical extension of the way America has chosen to live in the world. This war is the logical end of the American system that we've built, and I think that as young people who are being confronted with the choice of being in that war or not, we have an obligation to speak to this country, and that statement has to be made in this way: That this war will not be made in our names, that this war will not be made with our hands, that we will not carry the rifles to butcher the Vietnamese people, that the prisons of the United States will be full of young people who will not honor the orders of murder. . . ."

When he had finished his speech he strode out across the green field to an exit, like a man with no time to lose.

September 1967

Wendy Ewald

What's the future look like? It's the question that comes to mind at the sight of children in whatever impoverished place on this earth the camera finds them. What's the future look like for the youth in his flowery turban, over there in India? If he's an Untouchable, will that photograph transform him into a youth beyond caste, a youth transcendent? But what's the future, forty, fifty years beyond those gazing moments? Suppose somebody comes by with a camera again, will he say, *This is me when I was twelve, it's bent, you see, and faded, you see, but I kept it so you can see I was young once, like you,* and will the camera take its picture of him, whittled down to the bone, lacking some teeth, holding up the dim, cracked photo of himself in the flowery turban so the world can see that the two men are one and the same being? Shall we call it a worthy endeavor, Wendy Ewald's, bringing cameras to children who have none, so that, by taking pictures of themselves, they prove their existence, at least in their own eyes? But what's to become of those two sisters, artfully posed in the presence of a chopped-down tree that's sprouting fresh new leaves? They look like sisters but perhaps they're best friends in a place where neighbor marries neighbor, and no stranger wants in anyway, no jobs, no future. Will there be a neighbor, fifty years to come, who still has hidden in a drawer the little camera given her by a young woman who showed up one day with a big supply of cameras and rolls and rolls of film, and who gathered the children with her into a room called *the dark room,* where they saw themselves *oh look!* slowly, believably, coming to life on a simple piece of paper afloat in a magic solution? If there is that one neighbor with her camera, how will she pose those two sisters now? Side by side on a stoop, both heavily old, in their eyes their children's troubles? The television set, seen through the open door behind them, will have become their aperture onto the world, and that little camera will no longer surprise them with the inestimable value of their lives. That's what it must have done, that camera. A common toy for children of the privileged world, for Ewald's children the camera was a rarity that made a precious rarity of each and every child, the photographer and the photographed one. *But what's the future look like?* That's the question in the eyes, the faces, of children everywhere who are the Untouchables, the Unmentionables, and it's clearly present in these pictures, as varied as they are, like a light whose source is unknowable. Take the photo of the two girls dancing on the edge of the dried-up lake. It bears a distant kinship, a resemblance to Sebastião Salgado's photographs of the dispossessed, in Africa, in Central America, in Mexico, in India, in Cambodia, a vast everywhere on earth. Salgado takes us with him into a deeper reality. It's not just his kind of camera, one of the best, that does it, nor his film's unsurpassed sensitivity that finds a "visionary" light in the tragic grayness, in the denser darkness. It's something more and it's called compassion. With that, he imagines a different future in every harrowing scene, a time to come, when, in his words, *"all humanity will be concerned with the whole of humanity, all men with all other men, and that will be when we discover that compassion is the most important of all human qualities."* The child who took that picture, two friends dancing on the edge of a dried-up lake, must have caught a glimpse of that kind of future, a time when humanity will see to bringing change about: the lake bed filled to the brim with rainwater and spring water and flowing river water, and long-legged birds among tall, green rushes, wading around, stalking frogs, and a great number of shining fish, constantly passing one another as on promenade, way down in the lake's clear depths.

Winter 1997

The Last of Life

WHAT IT LOOKS like is a picket line against God. They are old, some very old, and they are dancing in the church, up there on the stage where on Sundays the pastor preaches, all holding a long, false vine of flowers, the women in diaphanous, pastel gowns and gold shoes, the men in chorus black and berets, and all singing, with their strained, untunable voices, WE LOVE LIFE AND WE WANT TO LIVE, demanding of Him what He has denied everybody so far. Below the red bow ties and the ribbons round the necks, the bodies, sashed and corseted, are deceptively similar to what they were decades earlier, the feet nimble, tricking the dictates of the baby grand; above, the faces are stunned by age, irretrievable. The spectators, some with mouths fallen open, not with enthrallment but with the stun of their own oldness, are in clothes from the Goodwill racks or else their own for half a lifetime. A lone young man, a derelict who has wandered in from the Tenderloin in whose center the Glide Memorial United Methodist Church is situated, mingles well.

Some are onstage for the first time in their lives and some were entertainers in their youth; a motley troupe, they are drawn together by age and by their need to publicly resist it, as if to perform for an audience is to force His attention, too. She's throwing roses to the front row, her black-feather picture hat back in use to adoringly frame her face, her fox-fur cuffs, almost as long as her gown, swinging again, her gold sandals, with little hourglass heels, in flirtatious touch with the stage that brings her again to life. Without the microphone her voice might sound like the chirp of a barely born bird. A couple of sailors and their girls in apricot gowns dance around one another; a buxom woman, twirling a black parasol, parades back and forth, declared to be Lillian Russell, at last fulfilling for herself the common wish to be mistaken for some famous beauty. Ages are sometimes called out, as if the performers are children and precocious. A chanteuse in a red, sequined dress that is slit high up the side to a bow promises great pleasures in Paris. A man in a tux, a woman completely in gold waltz together to his song: *In dreams I kiss your hand, Madame, your dainty fingertips/ Just when I hold you tight, Madame, you vanish with the night, Madame. . . .*

The Tenderloin is that section of downtown San Francisco where whatever may be undesirable for some is desirably concentrated for others. Black facade bars; barkers at the entrances of bars before flappy black curtains beyond which are the completely nude go-go girls; male and female hustlers, black and white; porno movies; dirty-book stores and dusty bookstores;

hotels that once had class and others that had none to begin. Eleven thousand of the city's old live in the downtown district that encompasses the Tenderloin, unable to afford the higher rents elsewhere that have risen with taxes and inflation and often prejudicially with the age of the tenant. Old women in the lobby of a Tenderloin hotel whose management caters to the old sit side by side of an evening on all the sofas, coats over knees, necks sinking forward as infants' do, staring out at the traffic. Some twenty chosen persons of the neighborhood, incapacitated for a time in body or spirit, are brought hot lunches in paper bags, prepared by Salvation Army volunteers and delivered by volunteers from the Council of Churches. But who are in all the rest of the rooms? One inmate, though she could be heard stirring around, failed to open the door to a friendly volunteer who left a calling card under the door on the first day and knocked every day for six days thereafter. At last, accepting this persistence as a sign of interest, she opened the door a crack.

Some appear more often. They come out to visit the O'Farrell Street Center, one of the many throughout the city called Senior Centers, granting at least the sound of respectability, even of prestige, to the old. A barbershop once, the center has display windows; but the members, growing less shy day by day, seem not to mind being observed. Across from me at the table where twelve or so sit over tea and cookies is a taciturn man who speaks only to say that he was born in Berlin, has lived in Palestine, and knitted and crocheted himself his jerkin of many colors, sectioned like a Mondrian. A thin, sallow man, in a black suit that is clean and pressed but whose fibers have sweated out the years, sits next to me. Seventy-six; his profile is biblical, his hair is thick and dark, he smiles almost always. Of Armenian descent, born in Boston, he came to the city in 1917. "I always worked," he says. "Always done a day's work. Then I went home and ate supper.

Then I went down to meet my roommate who had a shoe-repair shop."

"Take your spoon out. You'll stick it in your eye," cautions an old woman, passing.

White, opalescent edges circle the irises of his large-lidded eyes. The last job he had was fifteen years with a wholesale dry-goods company, taking orders, packing merchandise. He plays the tambourine in the center's six-piece orchestra. Vacuuming has begun, it is almost closing time. A male senior is pushing chairs to the side, vacuuming under the tables. Above the dreary roar the plump woman across the table goes on talking to me. Around her grey curls is bound an orange yarn; earrings almost as large as real oranges swing unceasingly; on her nails, gold polish. She wears tight yellow pants, a beaded black sweater. Her eyes appear to be embedded in blue suns comprised of blue swellings under, blue cosmetic on the lids, and the rays of a constant smile that is both skeptical and ingratiatory. Outraged over the communal toilet's overflow and the moldiness of the first hotel, where the rate for her room was $125 a month, she moved out to another, a little nicer. Once a week she treats herself to a $1.49 meal—steak, potatoes, green salad. "I was on *The Joey Bishop Show,*" she tells me several times. "I wore a red hat and a black velvet dress with white collar and cuffs." Her husband, dead now, was a realtor. Figuring she might not live to be sixty-five, she took her Social Security at sixty-two, losing almost twenty percent. We walk out together into the Tenderloin scene. Even in the cold wind her smile is fixed; her voice seems fleshed by the smiling cheeks. "I like the finer things in life," she says, her last words. The wind blows stronger at the corner where we part.

Over at the Glide, meanwhile, the Conference on the Aged is going on. In the Fellowship Hall, young and middle-aged delegates from around the country and the many old of the Glide's own Senior Center sit down together for refreshment: coffee or tea, pastry, a sliver of matzo. The Mistress of Ceremonies, an elderly woman who stands on a box to get close to the microphone and who, later, in the vaudeville, plays a child in a cape, reminds herself from the lined notebook paper: *Joke #1: etc. Joke #2: etc. Poem: Although the years bring aches and pains that render our muscles inert/ One consolation still remains, Thank Goodness our wrinkles don't hurt. A reminder that this is Passover. Jos. Addison said The essentials to happiness are something to do, something to love, and something to hope for. Blessing: Read from the napkin. Ivy Barnes' son passed away. Mr. Gadwake and the 1906 Quake. 9 boxes date nut toasties @ .82=etc.* It is a big dining hall with long tables, folding chairs, an upright piano. Somebody tears a sandwich in two and gives me half. The Chinese gentleman next to me, seventy-eight by his country's calendar, two years less by ours, hands me a poem from his briefcase, titled *Age,* that begins: *A man must be taught to be able to control his age/ And never let age control a man, said our Sage.* Rising every morning at five, he exercises every part of his body. "Trouble can start in a joint of the little finger." The delegates are introduced, rise to say a few words. A woman from Nashville urges them with her strong, authoritative voice to keep their "noggins alive." The grey matter on the inside, she tells them, is more important than the grey on the outside. Some faces seem not to be listening closely.

The delegates, by themselves later, confer about housing for the Aged of meager income. The Old are the most deprived of all groups — economically, to name only one kind of deprivation — and at the bottom of this heap are the Aged Blacks, more than familiar with discrimination and want. The White Elderly get used to these things a little later in life. In immense settlements of thousands, the Old live in mobile homes that are not going anywhere. Counties are erecting low-rent housing, though the choice is given to the residents around the selected site as to whether or not to permit such congregations. In these dwellings certain things for the peculiar welfare of the tenants must be considered: Suppose the tenant falls in the hallway. Will his arm be wedged between rail and wall? The space between is crucial. An alarm system should be installed in every room, and low enough so that the tenant, if only he can drag himself over to the button, can press it.

Is it a brand-new species, suddenly mutated, that must be reckoned with in all its characteristics, kept separate, observed, provided for? Their numbers seem to have taken everybody by surprise, even as old age has taken them by surprise, even as most spectacular problems seem to erupt, but almost never do, without warning. Councils — regional, national, churchly, secular — have been and are being organized. Institutes of Gerontology are now functioning at several universities, and one university in Los Angeles will have soon, if it has not already by now, a six-and-a-half-million-dollar research and educational center. In Baltimore is a four-and-a-half-million-dollar center for the study of the physiology and biology of aging, with hospital and laboratories. Conferences are constantly called, of Mayors' Committees, of Coordinating Councils, and the 8th International Gerontology Congress was held a year ago in Washington, D.C., to which twenty-one nations dispatched three thousand delegates.

MOST OF THE city's old are loners, their mates dead. To find a couple, in wedlock or not, is similar to penetrating into the wilderness for rare specimens. The couple I found are within walking distance of the Glide center but they choose not to walk that far. To go by bus would be a major task, and there is no incentive: they have each other. It's the only apartment house with a tree, she told me, to enable me to find it easily. The tree is very small, the building dingy, the apartments rented now, she tells me, to hippies and their dogs. She is eighty-five, he is eighty. They met in 1914, in the chorus of *Lady Luxury*. She lifts the sofa's seat, kneels down to the accumulation of photographs and newspapers in the secret compartment, under. When he bends over, without his cane, to the bin, his limbs shake uncontrollably. Up comes a New York *Morning Telegraph* for Sunday, May 19, 1912 — the red-bordered front page of the entertainment section, with the round face of Blanche Ring in a ring of eight other lovely young faces, among them the old woman's face when it was young; there is no resemblance. "Opened at the George M. Cohan Theatre the night the *Titanic* went down," she says. Up come the photos: himself in a stage uniform with white braid upon the chest and white-trimmed boots; himself in a tux, by a staircase, at his side a girl in a feather skirt and beaded blouse, gazing up at him with sweet longing. Others: in a touring car, a woman with a strong-will smile, a white bulldog beside her — Queenie Vassar, wife of Joe Cawthorn, the comedian. In fur coats and satin pumps, side by side in the same pose, the Fairbanks Twins, Madeline and Marian, eighteen, each with the same dark, heart-melting gaze. Max Dill, of Kolb and Dill, strutty in a white suit and vest and shiny black shoes. On the steps of an Atlantic City frame hotel: she and her sister in high-neck white blouses; a few steps below, their pompadoured mother who is the wardrobe mistress; others of the troupe; and a few male hotel guests. "Who's this?" he asks me. I don't know. "It's me," he says. The very large photo is of a handsome young man, posed, with the fine, equine tension of the actor, in a decor chair. On the tablecloth, crocheted when their son, dead now, was overseas in the Second World War, lies the scattered pile of photos, up from the sofa bin for one of the few perusals in the thirty years they have lived in this apartment. In the pile are pictures of more recent entertainers, of Bing Crosby, his young face like a doll's; of Clark Gable; of General MacArthur in a misfit frame; and a photo of a grave, laden with flowers, a low, iron fence around it — her father's in the British West Indies where, in Disraeli's time, he was an Acting Governor of Tobago.

Outside, the sounds of the wind. A cold stream of it comes down from the top of the window that does not close properly. On the ledge around the room: a painted plate of the tablets of the Ten Commandments and Moses in a shaft of light, arms raised; a white china rabbit; plastic Easter lilies. He sits at the table, remembering the names of the plays and the number of days in each city — Mobile, three days; Jacksonville, three days; Des Moines, three days; Chicago, months; Philadelphia, four or five weeks. Though he is beset by several ailments (on a stand by the TV is a shiny aluminum cake pan filled with medicine bottles), he is of good color, without wrinkles, his hair comparatively abundant; his eyes are clear, his voice strong; he hears all. She never sits still. From her transistor radio that she carries from room to room comes the constant metallic roar of the ball game. She coughs often, a deep, rumbly cough. Slender and tall, she wears a pale-blue sailor-collar dress, a blue ribbon around her head, a delicate gold bracelet. Her glasses magnify her eyes to theatrical proportions; when she removes the glasses for a moment, while telling me about the operation, her eyes appear shrunken, shapeless. Their Social Security was increased not long ago, his check from $65 to $75, hers from $113 to $130; but the amount of the increase has been deducted, by the state, from their Old Age Welfare. Food stamps are offered them by the Welfare Office, but in order to make use of them they would have to go by bus to the stores that honor them. As it is, they buy their groceries across the street. "They treat us right over there," he says. "They know us. They were youngsters when we moved in. On Saturday nights they give us greens that would wilt by Monday." One last photo—a troublesome one—no signature, the persons unnameable after half a century: a man in an over-coat and hat and a woman in a fur-trimmed coat and hat, stand-ing either side of a pedestal on which sits a baby in white.

At the door they tell me that a priest visits them once a month for communion. "They don't want old people in church. What if somebody collapses? What would they do with him?"

OTHERS, OLD, are habitués of the churches. In this city, the Council of Churches is the organizer of a network of centers, with the churches providing the facilities, the volunteers, and the funds. What do they do there, the Old? They make copper cuff links; tool key cases; play bingo; discuss current events; sing; exercise sitting up. They are informed as to which cafeterias and counters offer $1 meals for Senior Citizens. Sometimes they go on tours, of the F.B.I., of apple country. And out from the churches go friendly visitors to act as confidants. The churches (Catholic and Protestant) all work together—among them the Temple Baptist, the Old First Presbyterian, St. Anne's, St. Cecil-ia's, St. Joseph's, St. Peter's, St. Francis', St. Vincent de Paul's, St. Mark's, St. Mary's. The suicide figure begins to rise with age, after fifty, until in the decade between sixty-five and seventy-five it is three times higher than in the decade between twenty-five and thirty-five. Sometimes not even all the saints can help.

Would the number seem so great—twenty million, now, over sixty-five years and almost fifty million over sixty years—if it were not of discards but of the wise? The biological process of aging—one among its many manifestations being the loss of the organs' non-regenerative cells and their replacement by suffoca-tive fibers—presents itself as only another kind of imprisonment after a lifetime's variety both subtle and obvious. In line before me at the post office an old woman is buying stamps. A sheet of a new issue, called something like A Naturalist's Delight, is shown her: The American Bald Eagle; an African Elephant Herd; Dinosaurs in the Age of Reptiles. She slips it back to the clerk. "They're too wild," she says, "for old people." She and her friends will send their letters stamped with the safe faces of their Presidents. In the rear of the Greyhound bus depot, old men, all in hats, rummage in the trash cans for the day's newspapers, fold them, pack them away in the pockets of their suits to read, alone in their hotel rooms, the same old stories of assault, murder, trickery, famine, wars. A few among the Old are pointed out as exemplary, as it used to be done with a few among the blacks.

Unlike the blacks, whose integration may come soon, the Old, also a race apart and always growing in numbers, may have to wait for an altogether different time of Love, Peace, and Utopia.

May 1971

The Essential Rumi

IF YOU HAD *to spend the rest of your life on a desert island, what book would you take with you?* I'm being forced to the rail of an old sailing ship and I can't come up with an answer. I'm here at the rail of this century that's surely bound to go down into the darkest depths of human memory, and I'm given the chance to rescue one book before all's lost. I'm gripping the rail, knuckles white, and all I can do is deplore the life I've led, not shaping up, not reading all those books I should have read.

Some books I've only half-read, some I've partly read — called away by living voices, called away by others' lives, by my own voice wanting to be heard — and most I've read from cover to cover and even some over again, but they're not enough to choose from. And I can't even offer alternative proof of a highly selective kind of reading, a Ph.D., for example, bringing it out—is it parchment?—from an inside pocket, and I haven't any other kind of degree as evidence of considerable book learning.

Since I never trust facts, or declarations that resemble facts, I'm afraid if I name a book it will be taken for a fact, a hard fact, like those books chosen by erudite arbiters who choose the best, when, after all, the best is chosen only in those intensely intimate moments when reader and storyteller are utterly, blissfully alone together.

But even if the name of the one that was best for me were to come now to my lips, I couldn't reveal it. I'd be confessing an intimacy I'd rather keep sublimely secret. The books that are frantically signalling me won't do, either, even though they're longtime companions. I can remember our many meaningful engagements and how distressed I was when I discovered that one was lost, how I felt lost myself. Absence sharpens love and nearness strengthens it—with books as with the rest of us. And I've got a number of books close at hand in this small apartment—they've been transported in throw-away grocery boxes many times—but even if I had more time at this rail I wouldn't be able to choose one to take with me to that island, leaving the others to their fate, when I'd thought their fate was to be always at my side. I could give their names, but the only thing their names would reveal is the randomness of my reading, my roaming in libraries and used book stores.

In my teens, roaming the big Los Angeles main library, I could slip into any specialized room and get nose close to those impressive title-and-author spines all in a row. I could sidle in close to those great minds like a poor relation in a Russian novel, coming in and asking for a little upkeep, something to keep body and soul together. I could stand a long, long time in that narrow space between the bookcases, turning pages, reading. An outsider, longing to be a writer, wanting mentors, wanting confidants.

And maybe it was then, in those years, I first saw the homeless young man who later would appear in my story, "Who Is It Can Tell Me Who I Am," an unkempt, grim, and grouchy fellow, looking for the meaning of his life in the words of the poets he's taking from the shelves, an outsider like myself, imagining a home for himself there.

That library was destroyed, burned to the ground by an arsonist, and a brand new one has risen in its stead, but everywhere in the world other repositories of wisdom are going up in flames, and here I am at the rail and I can't name one book to take with me for solace. One won't do for solace. Then how about five, how about *The Dictionary of the History of Ideas* in five volumes? What a tribute to the human psyche, that attempt to locate the birthplace of an idea and trace its progress, its expansion and development, its compounding, its mutations, its failings and recoveries from mind to mind through the generations, at least up until the last date of publication before it went out of print.

But they'll be much too heavy for me to go overboard with; I'd sink before I ever reached that desert island. So maybe I'll choose a slim one, the poems of Rumi, say, and tuck him into that inside pocket, close to my heart. Over I'll go, praying I'll reach that island, praying it's really out there, maybe one of Melville's *Encantadas* — Enchanted Isles — even if it's only rock, only rock and seabirds, vast flocks, I hope, resting there.

Summer 1999

on writing

Acceptance Speech

*on Receiving
a second Gold Medal
from the Commonwealth Club
for the short story collection
Women in Their Beds
San Francisco, August 21, 1997*

THIS GOLD MEDAL given to me for my work takes nothing away from the value and the beauty in the work of other writers. Writing *is* work and, more often than not, it is hard work. One task is always to find the ideal meaning in each and every word we may want to use.

In ordinary conversation writers tend to be negligent, at times, like everyone else. They say "I mean, you know, is what I'm saying" or "You know what I mean?" and the listener usually doesn't. But writers shape up for interviews, and so I was surprised by examples of negligence in the words of an historian interviewed over the radio about his book on the Korean War.

The interviewer asked him why there were so few books on that war, and he said "Because the Korean War was nestled between two larger wars." Nestled? A child can be nestled, you can nestle a pet, say a cat or a dog, or a lover, but a war cannot be nestled, not any war, any place, any time. The historian went on to say that the Korean War was not a sexy war like the Vietnam War. Sexy? Can any war be sexy? Not with hundreds of thousands dead or maimed, not with all the suffering and terror. Perhaps the ideal word to describe a war is the word cruel. That cruel war, this cruel war. . . . The other day a judge in Brazil dismissed murder charges against four young men accused of pouring gasoline over an Indian tribal leader and tossing in the match. The Indian was asleep at a bus stop. The word murder in this case is especially relative: Who are these young men related to? One is the son of a federal judge and another the stepson of a former judge of the Electoral Tribunal. (It's unnerving to even say Electoral Tribunal.) The judge who dismissed the case called them good boys and said they were only playing. It will take a writer to get to the heart of the matter. It will take a writer to locate the meaning of the word good and the meaning of the word cruel, both words, in the life and death of Galdino Jesus dos Santos, a leader of the Pataxa tribe, who had traveled to Brasilia to join Brazil's largest demonstration ever in support of the rights of Indigenous Peoples and who lost his way in the city that night.

Now, at last, what is the meaning of the word Commonwealth? There are several ideal meanings, depending upon who is looking it up. The meaning it had for England was: Certain dependencies which all acknowledge the British Monarch as their head. That ideal meaning fell apart, it could not hold itself together. Naive as I am, I used to imagine that a Commonwealth meant a country whose wealth was held in common, an equitable distribution of that wealth. But that's an impossible ideal, you're not to give it a thought. The ideal meaning is found, I think, in the Commonwealth of Letters. The world's immeasurable and uncountable riches are held in common by the world's writers, whose most ardent wish, as they work, is to share that wealth with everyone else in the world.

Almost Impossible

SINCE I'VE BEEN trying for most of my life to make sense of myself with the works of my imagination and haven't yet accomplished that aim, how can I even begin to explain myself and make sense of myself this way, without my imagination to guide me? I'd rather conceal myself in that place where Thomas Merton longed to be, though it's understood I'll never make it that far and may not always want to be there: "If I have ever had any desire for change, it has been for a more solitary, more monastic way. But precisely because of this it can be said that I am in some sense everywhere. My monastery is not a home. It is not a place where I am rooted and established on earth. It is not an environment in which I become aware of myself as an individual but rather a place in which I disappear from the world as an object of interest in order to be everywhere in it by hiddenness and compassion." While hiddenness isn't the same as obscurity, it can lead you into obscurity, if that's the peril. Obscurity isn't so dreadful, after all, once you see that you're not the only one who's unknown, once you accept that you're as unknowable by the world as the world is unknowable by you.

When I began to teach, when I had to step onto center stage to make my living by being present as a writer, you can imagine the displacement I felt. Writing this essay is like being before a class again, struggling with that speechlessness that assails me whenever it's assumed I know what I'm talking about. So the only way I can manage this essay is as a response to those graduate students at Ohio University, benevolent strangers, even good samaritans, who went to the trouble of writing critiques of my short stories. I will always wonder why my stories seemed deserving of all that analyzing and theorizing, when to me my stories seem like visitors who I'm more than happy to embrace and who then begin to give me a troubled time, preying on my conscience, tormenting me with conundrums, then leaving at last for parts unknown.

There was some curiosity, in the essays, about the title of the collection — *The Infinite Passion of Expectation*. I'm curious about it myself. I can't remember where in Kierkegaard I found that ecstatic description of life itself. That's my interpretation of it, anyway. It's how we live, it's our very atmosphere and not just ours but every creature's, every seed's. We fix our expectations upon anything and everything — our next breath, of course, and our next heartbeat, upon persons, objects, endeavors, profits and pleasures, cataclysmic changes and transcendent ones, saviors of all sorts, and our immortal souls. It's a heavy title for so slight a collection.

On to the stories now, a few among those so minutely scrutinized and which I'm bringing into this essay only as hesitant guides to the person who dreamed them up. One student wrote of my "revealing that world which is only ever becoming and never actually present." Is that another interpretation of the infinite passion of expectation? My mother was blind. That graceful woman, whose energy was boundless and whose beautiful laugh I can still hear in memory, went blind expecting God to intervene and save her sight. A surgeon might have done it but she chose God because He's the one from whom you can expect the most. And so for the rest of her life, growing skinny and gray without seeing the change, she sat before her little mound-shape radio listening to those false dramas and waving her hand before her eyes, expecting it to take shape out of the dark. I was fourteen or so when the dark began to close in, and when I began to write did I expect to bring a shape, a meaning, even a reason-for-being from out the dark?

Is this perception by one student — "It's as if the ephemeral has found a concreteness in language that is more tangible than the realistic constructs of the story" — another clue as to why I began to write? Everything is ephemeral, as we all know, but some persons know it more. Was I so aware of it early on because I grew up in the Depression years and my father's jobs were never secure, and when my parents lost their home we went from pillar to post, and in one of those California bungalows we hung newspapers for curtains? What a sense of the ephemeral that decor must have imprinted in me. And I must have tried to save lives from vanishing by ensnaring them in stories, and to save the particulars of the Present from being swept away by the Past.

That's what writers are here for, but sometimes I think that the handwriting-on-the-wall we call graffiti may have more staying power than the most highly praised fiction of our time.

Some of my stories about women were written before the upsurge of the feminist movement and around the time I was reading de Beauvoir's *Second Sex,* and that great book parted the veils over my secret insights and perceptions and speculations and gave me the courage to tell about them. But my stories about women's plights are stories about men's, inseparably. "Myra" was written in a time when I was knocking on doors in a black neighborhood adjacent to my own, petition in hand for signatures to persuade the governor to save the life of a man on death row, and at one door I met the pregnant young woman who became Myra. The preciousness of the child in her womb wasn't apparent to the doctors or to the father or to the women for whom she ironed and cleaned house, and the baby was stillborn. One student essayist saw it this way: "Never again will she suffer in vain for hopes that rest with anyone else." Women come to this resolve more than once in their lives and so do men, as many times as crises and loss change us. In the story "Around the Dear Ruin," written in the time when abortions were illegal, the woman artist, small time, marries a merchant seaman for his wages, a man unloved by her, humiliated by her. She undergoes an alley abortion and dies. Baffled by her, he tells her young brother his feelings. "It's over me like a ton of water, the things I don't know." And when he lifts his head from the table, the red mark left on his brow is like a stigma, a sign of his ignorance of her depths.

Was it this unknowing of one another that led me to write the story "The Stone Boy"? About that boy, one student wrote of "his having to define a world he had not known existed." When the boy accidentally kills his brother, he enters a tragic world, a world not there before, and because that world is almost unbearable at first sight, he slips away for a brief time. He goes into the garden to pick the summer's yield, a chore he came out into the dawn to do, a chore that a farmer's son is expected to do, a chore he hopes will redeem him and bring him forgiveness. And I wonder — do we slip away from the tragic world for a brief time and even for a lifetime by going about our assigned tasks while the deprived and the denied and the homeless are all around us, and in an inquisition chamber, somewhere, everywhere, one person, man or woman or child, is alone with the enemy of us all?

Between the lines of every story readers write their own lines, shaping up the story in a collaborative effort, and that may explain why one student experienced a "strange terror" at the end of the story "God and the Article Writer" when I was elated by it and laughed a time or two as I was writing it. It gave me pleasure because I rescued a penny-ante writer from ignominy and subservience and confinement in his mind of facts and trivia. In the sixties I wrote articles for *Esquire,* interviewing persons of momentary interest and celebrities of sorts. Burley, my article writer, interviews a renowned physicist, Ancel Wittengardt, whose own view of Existence has been marvelously expanded by his recent discovery of the thirteenth-century Sufi poet, Ibn al-Arabi, a few of whose lines he recites for the uneasy interviewer. Such as "There is no existence except God. He is and there is with Him no before or after, nor above nor below, nor far nor near, nor union nor division, nor how nor where nor place. He is now as He was. He is the one without oneness and the single without singleness. He is the very existence of the first and the very existence of the last, and the very existence of the outward and the very existence of the inward. So that there is no first nor last nor outward nor inward except Him, without those becoming Him or His becoming them. He whom you think to be other than God, he is not other than God." Back in his dingy room in a residence hotel, Burley wakes into a state of astonishment. He does not yet know what astonishes him, and that's because he's part of it, like a fish in the sea, like a bird in the air.

Now about fears and wishes. There's the fear of being intimidated by anonymous authority, and by the not-so-anonymous, into giving up ideas that might be risky and contrary, and there's the wish to never give in or give up. There's unease over the times my eyes deceived me or my wits deserted me, and counterfeit ideas slipped into the work, and there's the wish that it never happen again. There's remorse over the time my conscience looked the other way, allowing a story to attempt a trespass on someone's inviolable depths, and there's the wish to be forgiven. And there's the wish that the delusion I labor under will never lift off and leave me. What a delusion! Imagining that I, too, can divide the light from the darkness.

1991

"Don't I Know You?"

An Interview with Gina Berriault

Bonnie Lyons and Bill Oliver

GINA BERRIAULT has been writing stories, novels, and screenplays for more than three decades. Best known and most honored as a short story writer, she has published two volumes of stories, *The Mistress and Other Stories* (1965) and *The Infinite Passion of Expectations: Twenty-Five Stories* (1982). Called "exquisitely crafted," and "without exception, nearly flawless," her stories are remarkable for their subtle craft and the variety of characters, settings, and subject.

Her first novel, *The Descent* (1960), is about a midwestern college professor appointed the first Secretary for Humanity, a Cabinet position designed to help prevent nuclear war. A plea for disarmament, *The Descent* depicts politicians militarizing the economy, harassing dissidents and promoting theories of winnable nuclear wars. *Conference of Victims* (1962), her second novel, explores the effects of the suicide of Hal Costigan on his family and mistress. *The Son* (1966), Berriault's third novel, is the account of the devastating effects of a woman's dependence on men for meaning in her life. This need to attract men eventually leads to a disastrous seduction of her teenage son. Her fourth novel, *The Lights of Earth* (1984), focuses on Ilona Lewis, a writer whose sense of self is undermined by the end of her relationship with a lover who has recently become a celebrity. Initially feeling unmoored, Ilona is finally drawn back into the world by the death of her brother, whom she has neglected.

In response to critics who have referred to Berriault's stories as "miniatures" or "watercolors," Berriault has said, "whenever I was referred to as a miniaturist or a watercolorist, I wondered if those labels were a way of diminishing a woman's writing. I believe that, now, because of the feminist movement, no reviewer would use those comparisons without hesitation." She added, "I hope my stories reveal some depths and some strengths, but if those virtues are not to be found in my work, then at least the intentions and the effort ought to call up a comparison with 12' × 12' acrylic."

Berriault also rejects any category more limited than "writer," saying, "I found my sustenance in the outward, the wealth of humankind everywhere, and do not wish to be thought of as a Jewish writer or a feminist writer or as a California writer or as a leftwing writer or categorized by an interpretation. I found it liberating to roam wherever my heart and my mind guided me, each story I've ever written."

Although she has received many fellowships and awards, is currently under contract with Pantheon for another story collection, and *The Infinite Passion of Expectation* has been called "the best book of short stories by a living American writer," we believe that Berriault's work has yet to receive the attention it deserves.

We talked with Gina Berriault in the Sausalito apartment of her daughter, Julie Elena. Although she was initially reticent about talking about herself and her work, her comments have the same honesty, depth, and humanity as her fiction.

BL/BO: How do you think your childhood reading affected you as a writer?

GB: That little girl who was me was a restless spirit, confined in a classroom and yearning to be out and roaming, either in the landscape or in her own imagination, and that restlessness was channeled into reading. I read more books than any other student in grammar school, roaming everywhere the persons in the stories roamed; I was those persons. Among the earliest books was *Water Babies* (that one belonged to the family across the alley and I remember climbing in through their kitchen window when they were away on vacation, reading it over and over, sitting on the floor in a corner) and George McDonald's great-hearted books, especially *At the Back of the Northwind* about a poor family and their love for one another. That deepened me. I began to know who I was, and that kids in poor families were worthy of books about them. And A.A. Milne, who wakened in me a delight in dialogue, an intuitive ear for what goes on between us and our beloved small animals — conversations of pretend naivete and subtle wit, that can make a child feel she knows more than adults think she knows. And later, in the novels of I. Zangwill, who wrote about Jewish families in Europe, I found a secret kinship, and I found that Jewish persons were worthy of being in novels. No one, all through my school years (except for a teacher who must have felt a kinship with Hitler) suspected that I was Jewish, and I must have been one-of-a-kind in that small California town. An insatiable reader, I began early to write my own stories, because, when you find yourself enthralled by their marvelous manipulation of language, when you find your wits sharpened, your heart stirred, your conscience revealed, then those writers become your guardian angels. They bring you to see your own existence as valuable — why else would they write their stories for you? — and they seem to be giving you their blessing to write your own. They seem to be blessing all children, even those who can't read a word.

Do you remember how you actually began writing?

My father was a free-lance writer for trade magazines and he had one of those old, stand-up-high typewriters. So I began to write my stories on it.

So you began writing when you were very young?

Yes, I began to write on that typewriter when I was in grammar school. I also wanted to be an artist and an actress. A drama teacher in high school offered to pay my tuition to an excellent drama school, but just at that time my father died and it was necessary for me to support my mother, brother, and sister. I never had any formal training as a writer, either.

Do you remember anything specific about how you taught yourself to write?

I simply wrote and wrote, and I was an avid reader. One thing I'd do was put a great writer's book beside the typewriter and then I'd type out a beautiful and moving paragraph or page and see those sentences rising up before my eyes from my own type-writer, and I would think "Someday maybe I can write like that."

You mean you'd type the words of someone else's story?

Yes, to see the words coming up out of my typewriter. It was like a dream of possibilities for my own self. And maybe I began to know that there was no other way for that sentence and that paragraph to be and arouse the same feeling. The someone whose words were rising from that typewriter became like a mentor for me. And when I went on with my own work, I'd strive to attain the same qualities I loved in that other person's work. Reading and writing are collaborations. When you read someone you truly love, their writing reaches your innermost self. You're soulmates.

How old were you when you did that experiment with your father's typewriter?

In my teens. I did it a few times. You shouldn't do it more than a few times because you must get on with your own.

Could you talk a bit more about how you began writing and publishing?

My experiment with my father's typewriter was going on at the same time I was writing my own stories. Rejection cards and letters with hastily scribbled encouragement helped to convince me that I existed. I remember a letter from an elegant, slick magazine, asking me to make a change or two and offer the story again. I did that, and when it was returned I cried for hours. By that time my parents had lost their house and the orange tree and the roses, and I wanted to earn enough with my writing to buy a farm for them. (I'd always wanted to live on a farm.) My father died before I could be of any help to him with my stories.

Elsewhere you mentioned that your mother began to go blind when you were fourteen. Could you talk about how that affected you as a person and as a writer?

As I wrote in my essay for *Confidence Women*, my blind mother sat by her little radio, listening to those serial romances and waving her hand before her eyes, hoping to see it take shape out of the dark. That could be a metaphor for my attempt to write, hoping to bring forth some light from out of the dark. I haven't yet.

How much formal education did you have?

After high school I took over my father's job. Then after work I'd roam through the Los Angeles public library and pick out whatever names or titles intrigued me. Having no mentor to guide me through that library, I just found writers by myself.

Do you regret not having a mentor?

My father was mentor for my spirit, I can say, and there were others from whom I learned about the world. I regret not having a formal, organized education. I wish I'd studied world history, philosophy, comparative literature, and I wish I'd learned several languages. Really, there is no excuse for my lack of those attainments, of that intellectual exploring, except as it is with every unschooled person — the circumstances of each one's life.

You don't say you regret not having gone through a creative writing program. Suppose a young writer wrote to you and said, "I admire your work and I want to write. Should I get a degree in creative writing?" What would you say?

I'd tell that person to learn more about everything, to rove, to be curious, and to read great writers from everywhere. If there's a true compulsion to write, a deep need, that person will write against all odds. And if that person enters a creative writing program, it would be for the purpose of learning how to shape what's already known and felt. Sometimes, when I taught workshops, I was glad I hadn't subjected myself to the unkind criticism of strangers. There's so much competitiveness, concealed and overt, among those who want to be writers and those who are writers. In Unamuno's *Tragic Sense of Life* he speaks about poets' desperate longing to be remembered, to be immortal. I think that concept of immortality is long past, long gone from our consciousness. Such immense change going on in the world, so much that will be irretrievable. So now the vying with one another is only for present gain. When I asked the students if they'd read this-or-that great writer, most had read only contemporary writers, and if the ads and the reviews praised those writers, the students accepted that evaluation. Ivan Bunin, for example, has been almost forgotten, and what a writer he was!

Speaking of contemporary writers, whose work do you admire?

Nabokov, Primo Levi, Jean Rhys — aren't they contemporary still? And to go a little further back, but still within my view contemporary, Chekhov, Turgenev, Gogol, Bunin. They are my first and last deep loves. I liked Raymond Carver's first collection best. Those stories were like underground poetry. He must have felt that the reader possessed an intuitiveness like his own, and picked up on the meaning, just as with poetry.

Isn't that a way of taking your reader as equal?

And when you take the reader as your equal, your work isn't affected or false. You establish that collaboration, that shared intuitiveness.

In your career there's a big gap between The Son *and* The Infinite Passion of Expectation. *Why?*

That's a question that should never be asked. It opens a wound. What can a writer say about gaps and silence? The question can't be answered because the answer involves the circumstances of a lifetime and the condition of the psyche at one time and another. How can a writer possibly answer it without the shame of pleading for understanding of one's confusions and limitations and fears? You call it a gap, but that's the time between publications. There is no measurable gap. I never ceased writing, but I destroy much of what I write or I can't work out what I want to say and I put the piece aside. The longing to write and the writing never cease. When I taught to make a living, evenings and years were given over to guiding students through their own imagination, to the neglect of my own. And there's the disbelief, so often at my elbow as I write, that I can write at all.

Do you see yourself primarily as a short story writer rather than a novelist?

Oh, yes. When my first stories were published, there was a lot of enticement from editors to write novels. But I wish I'd written twenty stories to one novel, instead. Short stories and some short novels are close to poetry, with the fewest words they capture the essence of a situation, of a human being. It's like trying to pin down the eternal moment.

Many critics have praised your work for the extraordinary variety of characters and settings, including characters of various races and classes. Do you think your life experience was important in developing that wide scope?

I never thought I had a wide scope. The way to escape from the person who you figure you may be is to become many others in your imagination. And that way you can't be categorized as a regional writer or a Jewish writer or a feminist writer, and even though you may be confined by the circumstances of your life, you're roaming out in the world, your imagination as your guide. I haven't roamed far enough.

You've said, "Between the lines of every story, readers write their own lines, shaping up the story as a collaborative effort." As the writer, are you concerned about controlling or directing the reader's lines, with the question of a "correct" interpretation?

Of course the writer wishes to compel and persuade and entice and guide the reader to a comprehension of the story, but there's no such thing as a "correct" interpretation of a piece of fiction. That's demanding a scientific precision of the writer. Each reader's interpretation originates in his or her life's experiences, in feelings and emotions of intensely personal history. You get more from what you read as you grow older, and your choices change, and, wiser, you bring more to that collaborative effort.

How about screenplays?

They're so mechanical to write, and you must leave out the depths you try to reach when you're writing your stories. A screenplay is a simplification and an exaggeration at the same time. By contrast, if you slip in a false note in a story, the whole thing falls. But a film can be packed with other persons' demands upon it, become a falsification of the writer's original idea, and then be hailed as one of the year's best — the usual. What makes a film work are the magnified, publicized, idolized actors moving around up there on the screen. And because the influence and the gain from movies are made to seem more real than from your obscure small stories, so many young writers think it's the highest achievement in life to write a movie script.

Were any of the interviews you wrote for Esquire *in the sixties memorable to you? To whom did you talk? In addition to your story "God and the Article Writer" did they have any lasting influence or effect?*

Whom did I interview? I interviewed the topless dancers, the first nightclub topless dancers, not first in the world, of course, but in San Francisco. I remember that an editor at *Esquire* asked me to write an article; they had published some stories of mine, and he said that fiction writers write better articles. So I offered the idea of the topless dancers, who had only recently stepped out onto the stages in North Beach. His "Okay" sounded tentative to me, and so I was very surprised when he phoned a few weeks later wanting to know where the article was. I had only a week in which to research and write, and I got it to them in time. Synchronicity is at work when you're writing an article. Pertinent things — overheard conversations, random meetings — are attracted by your task as by a magnet, and the article shapes up in a surprising way. That's not always the case, but it happens. Then an editor at *Esquire* asked me to interview someone or two who were fallen from the heights and so I found a very elderly couple, man and wife, who had been Broadway entertainers in their youth, and, in their shabby apartment, I looked through their piles of old newspaper clippings and photos; I was moved. I interviewed the student at Stanford who was a leader of demonstrations opposed to the Vietnam War, and I interviewed the men who were the firing squad executioners in Utah, the last firing squad that wasn't, after all, the last. They all wanted anonymity — shame, I suppose — and the photographer took their picture together in silhouette, dark, against a yellow sunset, out in a field. Since I am an outsider, an observer at heart, not an interrogator, I'm not facile at asking people about themselves. And protective as I am of my own secret self, my own personal life, I am reluctant to inquire of others, even though I find that some others don't mind at all telling about themselves. Pride intervenes, too; you feel subservient, at times, to the person you're interviewing, and it was this attitude, this uneasiness, this feeling of being an intruder, that brought about the story "God and the Article Writer," wherein the lowly article writer transcends himself by becoming one with God. It's a bit of a satire and it amused me as I wrote it.

In the more than thirty years you've been writing and teaching, what do you think has been the most significant change in fiction?

One thing that dismays is the cruel pornography of recent novels and how they're considered an honest probe of these desecrating times. What's inspiring is the work of more Black writers and Hispanic writers, and the availability of the small presses and quarterlies. But most of the short stories in most of the large circulation magazines seem about the same as they always were — about the middle class, their mishaps and misapprehensions. An elitism in a vacuum. There's no sorrow and no pity. We're far from writers like Steinbeck and Dos Passos and Nelson Algren. I remember reading *In Dubious Battle* all through the night, I remember just where I was and what period of my life — like a vivid fragment. There's been an intimidation of writers in this country. We write to be acceptable. Some things I wanted to write about, I haven't because I was afraid I wouldn't be published, and writing has been and is my livelihood. I supported myself and my child with my writing. I like to believe that I never misled and that I wrote truthfully, but I've always felt the presence of anonymous and not-so-anonymous authority.

Do you think there is a connection between the superficiality you find in so much writing today and the fact that many writers are academically trained and remain in academia as teachers?

It may be that superficiality results from covert or implicit censorship of our work. The academe isn't to blame, I think. Some very fine writers, prose and poetry, are teaching in universities to keep a roof over their heads and to find pleasure in teaching. Superficial writers seem to make a good living and don't need to teach.

Right now, a first person, present tense style is very popular. How do you feel about it?

I imagine that the first person, present tense is the easiest way to write. But to me it seems to contain the most emptiness. It brings a sense of immediacy, and with immediacy you think you've got hold of the truth and the real, and so there's a touch of satisfaction about it, a conceit. Just recently I was looking at Sebastião Salgado's book of photos, *An Uncertain Grace,* and there was a short introduction by Eduardo Galeano, who wrote "Salgado shows us that concealed within the pain of living and the tragedy of dying there is a potent magic, a luminous mystery that redeems the human adventure in the world." When I read that I thought that's what great writers have always done. Salgado lived in Africa with those suffering people and he lived in Central America. He was right there, where the truth and the real and that luminous mystery are found. It can all be found in this country.

Do you see yourself as a woman writer or as a writer who happens to be a woman? And has your gender affected your career at all, caused you any difficulties?

I've known and still know a fear of men's judgments and ridicule and rejection. At the same time I've been acutely aware of the oppression and abuse and humiliation that men endure and struggle against, the same that women endure and now know they don't have to endure. In other words, I'm a humanist, I guess.

How do you think of your work in relationship to the Women's Movement?

Most of my stories, early ones and later ones, are about women. My wonder and my concern over women are present always in the natural course of my writing.

When you look at your own work, do you think there are recurring themes?

I don't look over my past work, or I don't like to. I want to look over my future work. If there is a recurring theme, it's an attempt at compassionate understanding. Judgement is the prevalent theme in our society, but it's from fiction we learn compassion and comprehension. In Gogol's great story, "The Overcoat," there's a description of the poor copying clerk's threadbare overcoat, how the cold wind got in across his back. I don't know why those lines move me so much, except when you visualize how the cloth has worn out without his knowing until suddenly one day he's surprised by that cold invasion — isn't that a description of an entire life? That copying clerk is always ridiculed and insulted by the younger clerks. I guess that in my work, in my way, I attempt to rouse compassion for those who are called demented or alien or absurd or ridiculous, for those who are beyond the pale.

I think you do that wonderfully well in your work, especially with the brother in The Lights of Earth.

That *was* my brother, and though I told only part of the story, it was the most grueling work I've ever attempted.

Because it is about a woman writer, set in California, and many of the details seem to parallel your life, Lights of Earth *seems to be autobiographical. How autobiographical is that novel?*

Lights of Earth was an attempt to redeem and forgive myself, and maybe that's what autobiographical novels are all about. But it's impossible that characters and situations and scenes and plots be absolutely true to life. If you attempt that truth then you may be false to your creative spirit which knows how to handle truths in its own way.

Toward the end of Lights of Earth *when Ilona receives that healing letter from her daughter, Antonia, the narrator says "For a moment now the earth was hers to know, even as it was known to everyone to whom the earth with all its wonders appeared to belong. A child out in the world can do that for you, can bring you to belong in the world yourself." That second sentence seems to leave Ilona and speak to the reader about life in general in your own personal voice. Is that so?*

Yes, I suppose, and that's probably why, when you first came in and before the interview began, I spoke about my daughter. My child and my writing and others' writings and everyone I've loved, all have brought me to belong in the world.

It seems to me that although your writing is never propaganda, it is indirectly quite political and that you see social or political engagement as essential to serious literature. Do you agree?

Engagement is the only word you need, because it explains why some of us must write. And political engagement is essential to serious literature as design or perspective or materials are essential to any work of art, but only as an integral part of that engagement, that dedication.

What do you make of the idea, popular in some circles today, that writers should only write about people like themselves, people of their own ethnicity, class, gender, and sexual preference?

How limiting that is — to write only of your own ethnicity, class, gender, sexual preference. Your imagination is left to hang around the sidelines. Say that you're crammed in at a restaurant table with your ethnic friends or friends of the same preferences as yourself, all speaking the same language, and you notice someone, a stranger, out on the street, who's glancing through the window, and your eyes meet his, and you want to get up and go out and say to that stranger, "Don't I know you?"

afterword

The Achievement of Gina Berriault

Richard Yates, 1979

FOR MORE THAN twenty years now, Gina Berriault has been writing remarkably sensitive and powerful fiction. Her style is lucid, lyrical and very much her own, and she seems to have any number of strategies for breaking your heart.

The first Gina Berriault story I ever read, long ago, let me know at once that I would never forget it. It's called "Around the Dear Ruin," and this is how it opens:

> My sister married Leo Brady because he was a merchant seaman and made good wages, and because he was gone most of the time. She and her five-year-old boy had been living on the sales of her cable car etchings that tourists to

San Francisco picked over in the little art galleries and bookstores, and on the sporadic sales of her oil paintings. They were married a few days after he came from sea, and a week later his ship sailed again for the Orient. In the six weeks he was away, the steamship company sent her, at his request, all his wages. But the day that he returned was unrewarding for Leo.

Clara had her studio in an old building on Columbus Street. The first floor was occupied by the Garibaldi Club whose members assembled every evening for cards; above her, on the top floor, lived two young men, a bank clerk and a window dresser. But she knew Leo's step on the bottom stair and, lifting her head from the pillow, she said, "Why couldn't his ship have cracked in two? All the others did."

I was kneeling to help Mark, her boy, undress for bed, and I paused with my hands at his waist and lifted my head to hear her above his prattling. "Did you want anything?" She had been lying in a fever all day.

"Listen, listen!" she admonished me.

And I listened and heard the steps.

Clara Ruchenski, a gifted and fiercely ambitious young painter, is lying in a fever because, on finding herself pregnant by Leo, she has gotten a cheap, bungled abortion, has refused hospital care and will soon die — though not before suffering great pain and losing her mind.

Clara may once have seen Leo Brady as "a big, sweet guy with a respect for artists," but that's all over now; what little is left of her life is consumed in detesting him and cursing her fate.

After her death, and after Leo has sprinkled her ashes in the redwood grove where he first kissed her (secretly saving a pinch of the ashes to carry with him in a tiny enameled box), Clara's paintings are exhibited in a prestigious gallery, to wide acclaim. And so a solemn, reverent cult of admirers comes to entwine itself around the dear ruin of her life — as often happens when an artist dies young — but this is of little consequence or comfort to Leo.

The narrator of the story is Clara's younger brother Eddie, also a painter, whose love for his sister is understated but made achingly clear on every page. With Clara dead, Eddie finds he is always uncomfortable around his bumbling, grieving brother-in-law, though he makes a point of keeping in touch and of asking Leo over whenever his ship ties up in San Francisco. During one such visit a year or more after the death, as the two men make awkward conversation at the breakfast table, Leo suddenly brings out and displays the enameled box.

> With false aplomb he bounced the box in his hand in an attempt to forestall his collapse, for his voice was breaking and falling in his chest. . . .
>
> "She's in the palm of my hand," he said. "That's why I kept this. She's harmless and she's amenable. She's nothing. If I took the ashes between my fingers, it would powder off into air. But I'm alive, God damn it, and that means something. There's a big difference between alive and dead, they can talk big all they want about how life is so meaningless. This hand, it's alive, and it's patted the rumps of a lot of pretty women since Clara died. She's only a pinch of snuff. . . . This is what they come to," he said, shaking so much that he had to stand up, and precisely he set the box down by the salt and pepper shakers. "This is what they come to. They're the stupid ones. They go crazy. They go crazy and eat dirt."
>
> Jerking the chair far out with an elaborate gesture, he sat down again, pressing his forehead against the table's edge. After a while he spoke to the floor: "It's over me like a ton of water, the things I don't know."

And that eloquent line is the story's conclusion.

This brief summary can't possibly do justice to it, but you can find the whole of "Around the Dear Ruin" in Gina Berriault's collection *The Mistress and Other Stories* (1965), along with fourteen further examples of her superb skill at short fiction. One of them is "The Stone Boy," perhaps the best known and most widely anthologized of her stories, in which a farm boy's profound shock on accidentally killing his brother is misinterpreted by everyone as callousness. Another, "The Birthday Party," relates the final stages of a young woman's unhappy love affair from the viewpoint of her seven-year-old son, who isn't supposed to know what's going on.

Miss Berriault has also published three novels, with a fourth promised soon. Her first, *The Descent* (1960), could be called a political allegory. Arnold Elkins, an idealistic professor of history, accepts a U.S. President's appointment as "Secretary for Humanity," assuming he will work for world disarmament. Instead he finds himself baffled and ignored at every turn: Nobody wants to hear his ideas because nobody's interested in disarmament anyway. The nuclear arms race is all the rage, bigger and better bomb shelters are a source of dizzying civic pride, the armed forces have elected a glamorous girl to be "Miss Massive Retaliation." The scenes of Arnold's frustration, discomfort and weariness shift from Washington to the U.N. to Hiroshima, and then to long, low-budget traveling around the United States. His eventual downfall, which comes about through a series of increasingly gross misunderstandings, seems forced and thus unconvincing, but that's an occupational hazard in books like this — novels conceived and born in political anger. I've never believed the ending of *1984*, either. Still, there are fine things all through *The Descent*: sharp characterizations, notably of Arnold's wife and adolescent daughters, and vivid evocations of the urban American land-scape — bus stations, construction sites, third-rate hotels.

With her second novel, *Conference of Victims* (1962), the author returns to the stuff of her short stories. Here, and in the rest of her published work to date, there is no more straining of plausibility.

A bright and popular young California man, running for Con-gress, has committed suicide. He was married and a father, and so it's generally assumed that he killed himself in fear of profes-sional ruin following a rude public disclosure of his affair with a high-school girl. These circumstances set the novel in motion. In long sections, each of them rich and self-fulfilling enough to be a story in its own right, we then explore the lives of the dead man's survivors, the "victims" of his final act: his widow, his mother, his sister and younger brother — and the high-school girl, whose name is Dolores Lenci, and who I've always consid-ered one of Gina Berriault's finest creations.

Few things in modern fiction have moved me as powerfully as what happens to this girl after she has left her home town for San Francisco, where she shyly hopes to consolidate a new sense of herself as being greatly desirable — the image born of the doomed candidate's love for her. She finds work as a waitress and is almost at once taken up by a wealthy, boastful, fifty-year-old building contractor, a childless man whose wife is independently successful in business too. Dolores doesn't much like him — she spends a lot of time covertly observing his every frailty and the nervous fumbling in his every show of self-importance; she also comes to resent his parsimony in failing to provide her with nice gifts and an apartment of her own. But she has to acknowledge a "disturbingly pleasant feeling that she (is) more desirable than the wife," and soon she finds she is afraid of losing him because he has become "more familiar to her now than any man had ever been."

Late one night, as they lie in a cheap beach cabin he has brought her to, she begins to cry and tries to tell him about the young politician's death.

"There was a man who killed himself over me," she wept. "You think I'm nobody, but there was a man who fell in love with me and killed himself. You think I'm nobody."

"No, hell, I don't think you're nobody," he snuffled, patting her belly. "What do you mean, he killed himself," patting.

"I mean what I said!" But it ought to be told, she thought, as an actress would tell it, walking through a meadow or along the beach with the man tall and listening and with love in his eyes and sympathy for the anguish of her memory. . . .

"He was married," she said, "and he had a little boy," covering her mouth with her fingers that were wound around with her hair.

"Yuh, go on," patting.

"He knew we were going to be found out, but he didn't care. . . ."

"Yuh?"

"He didn't care."

He was silent, patting. "Listen, sweetie, listen, doll," he said. "You must have left something out."

"What?"

"You tell *me* what," he said. "I don't want to hurt your tender feelings, but it doesn't seem like that's enough reason for a man to kill himself about."

"You don't know the whole story," she cried.

"That's exactly what I'm saying," he told her.

"He was running for Congress," she explained with as insulting, indignant enunciation as she could scare up for her small, broken voice, "and we were found out a few days before election day. What I'm saying is that he didn't care about the election, he didn't care what was going to happen, I mean if he had to kill himself because of the scandal. What I'm saying is that he couldn't help it if he was in love with me." But it sounded like the elaborate lies she used to tell when she was a little girl. . . .

"Sounds funny to me," he said. "Oh, you're telling the truth all right, you're telling the truth as you see it. But a man doesn't do that, I mean go out of his mind for wanting some girl unless he's out of his mind already." He turned his back on her again to tie his shoes. When he straightened up he consulted his wristwatch. . . .

She placed a palm over her nipple to hide the sudden small spangle of pain that she thought was audible to him. It was a voice she didn't want him to hear, it spoke without asking her if it could. He had taken away from her whatever it was she had tried to claim for herself in this story . . . he had taken it away from her with his mockery of it, the voice calling to him to remind him that he was wanted, that without him she had no voices to listen to.

He dropped her underwear and slip over her breasts and over the crossed hands. "Come on, come on," he said. "What you looking like a madonna for? You Catholic? Come on, come on. You sore at me because I said your story didn't make sense?" He switched on the paper-shaded lamp, dropped her dress over her stomach, covering up everything he had wanted uncovered before. He was amiable about it all, like a good boss who jokingly prods his employee to work faster to demonstrate how fond each was of the other. Her nylons he dropped on her thighs.

"You're not so great," she heard herself say low.

"Hell, I know I'm not so great," he said, pretending surprise, pretending good humor about his deficiencies. . . .

She tossed aside the clothes with angry flicks of her hand and sat up and began to dress. "You're not so great."

"Nobody ever told you I was, did they?"

. . . She glanced up as she dressed and saw her reflection in the window that he was peering through. The image of the half-clad girl was imposed between him and the darkness. . . . With her dress held to her breasts she paused to stare at his back, at his gray head bent forward so the brow touched the glass, and at her almost transparent self in the pane. . . . No, this one was not so great and the other one had been not so great, they were all dying, and the tall, long-haired girl in the glass was a gift and not to be paid for, a gift that they claimed as their due, something owed them by life. But the girl herself, the girl herself, who was she? The girl made of reflection and glass and night, who was she to herself?

He turned and stood waiting with his back to the window, his hands in his pockets jingling coins and keys. They said nothing more to each other and she saw when she glanced once at his face and found him gazing at nothing, at the rug, that the taste of the end filled his mouth as it did her own.

In common with James Jones, Gina Berriault knows that ill-educated or inarticulate people are as sensitive as anyone else. She renders their speech with a fine and subtle ear for the shy or strident inaccuracies, for the bewilderment of missed points and for the dim, sad rhythms of cliches; but when she takes us into the silence of their minds, their thoughts and feelings come out in prose as graceful, as venturesome and precise as she can make it. That's a rare ability, and reflects a rare degree of insight. It may well be one of the most valuable skills a writer can learn — which makes it disappointing to discover, time and again, how few of the most celebrated novelists have bothered to learn it at all.

The Son (1966) is an extraordinary performance. Technically and structurally, it surpasses both of Miss Berriault's earlier novels. In the combination of swiftness and complexity, it suggests the quality of her best short stories.

Once again a story of California — and no writer working today has a better sense of that warm and dismaying place — the book follows an attractive woman named Vivian Carpentier from a privileged girlhood into an emotionally desolate middle age. An early, romantic, quickly dissolved marriage leaves her with a son to raise alone, and she does the best she can. But Vivian has many lovers while her child is growing up — men who change her, either by enhancing her life or depleting it — and so by the time the boy comes to manhood we are prepared to expect some dreadful collision between mother and son.

This narrative is so fluid and its scenes so interdependent that perhaps no single excerpt, if printed here, would convey the spirit and power of the whole. But get the book if you can. There isn't a dull sentence in it or a moment's error in phrasing or tone — and the shock of its climactic episode, which in lesser hands might easily have fallen into sensationalism, is a triumph of writing at its purest.

As her many faithful readers must certainly have felt and said for years, there ought to be a much larger audience for Gina Berriault's work. An awful lot of people are fooling around with "creative writing" in America today, and they often turn up on the best-seller list, but this woman is the real thing. She has, along with all the other hard-earned virtues of her profession, something to say.

I think she is telling us what the great writers of the past have always wanted us to understand: that ignorance and terror are never far from possession of our hearts, and so at any time it may be over all of us, "like a ton of water," the things we don't know.